The Other Room at Porter's

AMERICAN NIGHTMARE

by/gan Matthew **Bulgo**

CAST:
Clara: Ruth Ollman
Greg: Chris Gordon
Daria: Lowri Izzard
Elwood: Gwydion Rhys
The Program: Richard Harrington

CREATIVES:
Writer: Matthew Bulgo
Director: Sara Lloyd
Designer: Delyth Evans
Lighting Designer: Katy Morison
Sound Designer/Composer: Tic Ashfield
Videographer: Simon Clode
Production Manager: Rhys Williams
Stage Manager: Hattie Wheeler
Fight Director: Kev McCurdy
Associate Director: Matthew Holmquist
Assistant Director: Duncan Hallis
Casting Director: Nicola Reynolds
Accent Coach: Emma Stevens-Johnson
BSL Interpreter: Sami Thorpe
Set Builder: Will Goad
Production Photographer: Kirsten McTernan

FRONT COVER IMAGE:
Photography: Aenne Pallasca
Design: Limegreentangerine

American Nightmare was first performed at The Other Room, Cardiff from 10/09/2019 – 29/09/2019. It was commissioned and produced as a part of The Violence Series.

TheOtherRoom
at Porter's

Artistic Director & CEO: Dan Jones
Producer: George Soave
Associate Director: Matthew Holmquist
Trainee Director: Nerida Bradley
Trainee Producer: Ben Clark
Press & Marketing Associate: Alys Hewitt
Executive Producers: Dan Porter & David Wilson

The Other Room at Porter's is Cardiff's pub theatre. It was founded by Artistic Director Kate Wasserberg and Executive Director Bizzy Day in response to the exciting opportunity to develop an audience for drama in the heart of Cardiff. An intense, purpose-built space with 47 seats, The Other Room produces great modern plays and new work by and with Welsh, Wales-based and Wales-trained artists. The Other Room has fast established a reputation for quality and daring drama, won Fringe Theatre of the Year at the 2016, Stage Awards, and a plethora of accolades at The Wales Theatre Awards in 2015, 2016 and 2017. The theatre was shortlisted in the Arts category of the Cardiff Life Awards 2017 and 2018, as well as for the prestigious Peter Brook Empty Space Award, 2017. The Other Room is currently run by Artistic Director and CEO, Dan Jones.

The Other Room would also like to thank Arad Goch, Arts Council England, Arts Council of Wales, The Carne Trust, Claire Bottomley, David Bond, Emily Pearce, The Esmee Fairbairn Foundation, The Garfield Weston Foundation, Hayley Burns, Heather Davies, The Leche Trust, Michael Carklin, National Theatre Wales, Philip Carne, Pontio Arts and Innovation Centre, Porter's, Prysg, Royal Welsh College of Music and Drama, Samantha Jones, Theatr Clwyd, Theatrau Sir Gâr, Theatre503, Theatre Genedlaethol Cymru, University of South Wales, Wales Millennium Centre and Yasmin Williams.

Special thanks to **Bizzy Day** for her work on American Nightmare as Producer and Fundraiser (January 2018 – June 2019).

Writer's Thanks

Nick Quinn, Alfie Coates and everyone at The Agency

Dan Jones and everyone at The Other Room

Dan Porter and everyone at Porters

James Illman, George Spender and everyone at Oberon Books

Sara Lloyd for wrangling the beast

Tic Ashfield, Ben Atterbury, Nerida Bradley, Ben Clark, Simon Clode, Bizzy Day, Delyth Evans, Will Goad, Chris Gordon, Duncan Hallis, Richard Harrington, Matthew Holmquist, Alys Hewitt, Lowri Izzard, Limegreentangerine, Kev McCurdy, Kirsten McTernan, Katy Morison, Ruth Ollman, Aenne Pallasca, Gareth Pierce, Matthew Raymond, Nicola Reynolds, Gwydion Rhys, RWCMD, George Soave, Othniel Smith and the cast of 'The Language of Violence', Emma Stevens-Johnson, Georgia Theodoulou, Sami Thorpe, University of South Wales – The Atrium, Wales Millennium Centre, Rhys Williams, Kate Wasserberg, Hattie Wheeler.

And above all, Elin Phillips for her constant support and patience of a saint.

Apologies to anyone I may have neglected to include on this list.

MB

WRITER: Matthew Bulgo

Matthew Bulgo trained at LAMDA and works as an actor, playwright, dramaturg and tutor.

Credits as a playwright include: *#YOLO* (National Theatre, NT Connections); *Constellation Street* (The Other Room); *Last Christmas* (Dirty Protest/Theatr Clwyd) which transferred to the Edinburgh Fringe, Soho Theatre and the Traverse Theatre; *The Awkward Years* (The Other Room/ Chapter); *The Knowledge* (Dirty Protest/Royal Court, 'Surprise Theatre' Season); *My Father's Hands* (Paines Plough, Come To Where I'm From); *Lacuna* (Three Streets Productions, New Wimbledon Studio); *Real Human Being* (Taking Flight Theatre).

He was the recipient of the Best Playwright award at the Wales Theatre Awards 2015 for his debut play *Last Christmas* and received the accolade again in 2017 for *Constellation Street* which also picked up the award for Best Production.

He is an Associate Director of Dirty Protest.

CAST:

Clara: Ruth Ollman

Ruth Ollman grew up in Cardiff, and graduated from Guildhall School of Music and Drama in 2017.

Theatre credits include: The Governess – The Turn Of The Skrew (Clapham omnibus) Lisa – All The Little Lights (Home Studio, Finsbury Park), Lydia – Still Alice (U.K tour), Sian – August (GSMD)

Film/TV credits include: Hazel – Love spreads (Jamie Adams) Leila – Pink Wall (Tom Cullen) Yvonne – The Last Summer (Jonathan Jones) Kimmy – Hymns & Ariyas (Jamie Adams)

Greg: Chris Gordon

Television includes: Regency (Nazimo Productions); Casualty (BBC); The Crown (Netflix); Silent Witness (BBC); Vera (ITV); Father Brown (BBC); Poirot (ITV); and Stella (Sky).

Theatre includes: The Winter's Tale (Cheek by Jowl); Romeo and Juliet (Sherman Theatre); The Lower Depths (RWCMD); Incomplete and Random Acts of Kindness (RWCMD); Anne Boleyn (RWCMD); Beast & Beauties (RWCMD); and Vincent in Brixton (RWCMD).

Daria: Lowri Izzard

Lowri graduated from RADA in 2016.

Theatre credits include; Lord of the Flies (Sherman Theatre/Theatre Clwyd), Votes For Women (New Vic Theatre), A Midsummer Night's Dream (Wiltons Music Hall), I Capture The Castle The Musical (Watford Palace/Oxford Playhouse), The Tempest (The Orange Tree Theatre) and Much Ado About Nothing (Faction Theatre).

She also appears as PC Mari James in series 1 & 2 of "Hidden/Craith" for BBC & S4C.

Workshop credits include; The Boy In The Dress (The RSC), Saint George and the Dragon (National Theatre), Maid of Orleans (The Bunker Theatre).

Elwood: Gwydion Rhys

TV Credits include: Hinterland (BBC), Hidden (BBC), 35 Diwrnod (S4C), Parch (Boom), Cara Fi (Touchpaper Tv), Tir (Joio TV).

Stage Credits include: To Kill a Machine (Scriptography Productions), Only The Brave (Soho Theatre / WMC), The Village Social (NTW), Crazy Gary's Mobile Disco / Pornography (Waking Exploits), Little Wolf (Lucid Theatre), The Wood / One Man Two Guvnors (Torch Theatre), Three Nights Blitz (Swansea Grand Theatre).

The Program: Richard Harrington

Richard Harrington's work in theatre includes Home I'm Darling (National Theatre & Theatr Clwyd); Duke Of Yorks, Coriolanus and The Persians (National Theatre Wales); Look Back in Anger (Theatre Royal Bath); Other Hands and Art and Guff (Soho Theatre); Stone City Blue (Theatre Clwyd), Gas Station Angel, House of America (Royal Court).

TV includes Endeavour, Gangs Of London, Hinterland, Death in Paradise, Requiem, Inspector George Gently, Father Brown, Poldark, Wolfblood, Lark Rise to Candleford, Land Girls, New Tricks, Bleak House, Dalziel and Pascoe, Spooks, Hustle, Rehab, Care, Silent Witness and Gunpowder, Treason & Plot.

Film includes Gwen, The Last Summer, Just Jim, Elfie Hopkins, Burton: The Secret, House Of America and The Contractor. Radio includes One Horizon, The Kraken Wakes, The Aeneid, A Child's Christmas in Wales and Antony and Cleopatra.

CREATIVES:

Director: Sara Lloyd

Directing Credits include Nyrsys (Theatr Genedlaethol Cymru) Anweledig (Frân Wen) Merch yr Eog (Theatr Genedlaethol Cymru) Rhith Gân (Theatr Genedlaethol Cymru/Eisteddfod Genedlaethol Cymru) Swansea's Three Night Blitz (Swansea Grand/Joio) The Ugly Duckling / Yr Hwyaden Fach Hyll (Sherman Cymru/Theatr Genedlaethol Cymru) Dŵr Mawr Dyfn (Sherman Cymru/Theatr Genedlaethol Cymru/Eisteddfod Genedlaethol Cymru) Pridd (Theatr Genedlaethol Cymru), Leaves on the Line (Royal Court/Dirty Protest) Under the Sofa/Breathe (Almeida/Dirty Protest). 'Fala Surion (Cwmni'r Frân Wen) and Tân Mewn Drain (Sherman Cymru).

Her work as a dramaturg includes the opera Y Tŵr (Music Theatre Wales / Theatr Genedlaethol Cymru) and the dance piece Babalus (ICoDaCo) tour of Wales and Sweden. Associate Director Credits Include Cyrano de Bergerac (Theatr Clwyd) and she is a former Associate Director at Theatr Genedlaethol Cymru.

As an actress Sara has worked at Theatr Clwyd, Salisbury Playhouse, Sherman Theatre, Theatr Genedlaethol Cymru, her television credits include Bang, Hinterland / Y Gwyll, Gwaith Cartref, The Indian Doctor.

Designer: Delyth Evans

Delyth trained at The Royal Welsh College of Music and Drama, graduating in 2018. Recent credits include How We Begin (King's Head Theatre), One Giant Leap (Brockley Jack), In Lipstick (The Pleasance Theatre), Out of Love (LAMDA), All That (The Kings Head) and Punk Rock (RWCMD).

Lighting Designer: Katy Morison

Katy is a Lighting Designer based in South Wales. She has recently worked on Shooting Rabbits/Saethu Cwningod by Powderhouse and Woof at Sherman Theatre, which follows her Christmas season at the venue lighting both Alice in Wonderland and Little Red Riding Hood/Yr Hugan Fach Goch. Her work in 2018 included Exodus for Wales-based company Motherlode and follows from the success of The Good Earth, which received 5-star reviews and enjoyed an off-Broadway run in New York to critical acclaim. She also designed three shows as part of National Theatre Wales' NHS70 season.

She has worked as an associate and Re-lighter, as well as Lighting Designer for Venue 13 at the Edinburgh Fringe, and also as a Production Supervisor and lighting tutor at Royal Welsh College of Music and Drama.

She was a member of the Production Team at Sherman Cymru for over 7 years.

Sound Designer/Composer: Tic Ashfield

Tic Ashfield MMus BMus (Hons) (RWCMD) is a BAFTA Cymru Award Winning Composer and Sound Designer based in South Wales. She has created music and sound for numerous projects including work for film, TV, theatre, dance, animation, installation and educational outreach projects. Commissioners and collaborators include BBC 1 Wales, BBC 2, BBC 4, S4C, All3Media, Fiction Factory, Severn Screen, John Hardy Music, Creative Assembly, National Theatre Wales, The Other Room Theatre, Taking Flight Theatre, Chippy Lane Productions, Omidaze Productions, Winding Snake Productions, Welsh National Opera, Lighthouse Theatre, Joio and Gwyn Emberton Dance.

As a composer and sound designer she focuses on using a combination of found sound manipulation and sampling, synthesis and instrumental writing to create bespoke soundworlds, often within collaborative settings.

Videographer: Simon Clode

Simon is an artist/filmmaker whose work intercuts many disciplines, with interests lying in ethnographic, environmental and global political commentary. His films have screened in competition at BAFTA qualifying festivals such as Aesthetica Short Film Festival. Arts Council Wales supports his artist films with his recent film installation showing at the Qalandiya International. He is one of the directors selected for the BFI Network / BAFTA GURU 2019/2020 program, as well as being a BFI Horizons recipient.

Production Manager: Rhys Williams

Rhys worked in the Audio Visual industry for over 25 years with responsibilities in deploying worldwide systems and solutions to many corporate giants. In 2018 Rhys decided to change career to follow his passion in the Theatre and Live Events. Since making that decision, Rhys has undertaken a Master's Degree at the Royal Welsh College of Music and Drama in Stage and Event Management. Rhys has worked on many Theatrical and Live Events, from technical support through to site coordination assistant and now enjoys the challenges brought by Production Management.

Stage Manager: Hattie Wheeler

Hattie graduated in 2016 from the University of Exeter, gaining a BA (Hons) in History. During her time at university she was heavily involved in theatre becoming the president of the musical theatre society. In 2017, she then went on to study Professional Stage Management at the Bristol Old Vic Theatre School, graduating in 2019. Previous Credits include: The Life and Adventures of Nicholas Nickleby (Bristol Old Vic), The Caucasian Chalk Circle (The Tobacco Factory), Let the Right One In (Circomedia), Clybourne Park (Bristol Old Vic Studio), Mad Forest (Wickham Theatre), Tender Napalm (Wardrobe Theatre).

Fight Director: Kev McCurdy

Kev is an Equity professional Fight Director. He primarily trained as an actor at The Royal Welsh College of Music and Drama from 1991 – 1998. He gained his Equity Professional Fight Directors status in 1996. Kev has been Royal Welsh Colleges' resident fight tutor since 2005 and has worked on a variety of stage, tv and film projects around the UK and abroad. Kev was also very honoured to have been awarded The Paddy Crean Fight Award at the event 4 years ago. He was also awarded the RWCMD Fellowship award 2 years ago. He's also the Co-Founder and Chairman for The Academy of Performance Combat. Kev has worked on numerous plays, tv shows, operas, video games and feature films. Some companies he has worked for: Walt Disney, Pixar, Atlas Entertainment, RSC, National Theatre, Old Vic, Young Vic, Shakespeare's Globe, Curve Theatre, Manchester Royal Exchange, BBC, Sky 1, ITV, Channel 4, S4C Wales, Sega.

Associate Director: Matthew Holmquist

Matthew is the current Associate Director at The Other Room Theatre as well as Artistic Director of Red Oak Theatre.

Directing credits include: *Cardiff Boy* (Red Oak Theatre, The Other Room) *A Recipe for Sloe Gin* (Clocktower Theatre, World of Boats), *Blue Stockings* (Sherman Players, Sherman Theatre), *The River* (Red Oak Theatre, Loco Bristol); *We Had a Black Dog* (Red Oak Theatre, Theatre De Menilmontant, Paris).

Associate Director/Staff Director credits include: *Eugene Onegin* (Buxton Opera) *Le Vin Herbe, Don Giovanni* (Welsh National Opera / Opera Cenedlaethol Cymru); *A Christmas Carol* (Simply Theatre, Geneva).

Assistant Director credits include: *Tremor, Taming of The Shrew* (Sherman Theatre) *Simplicius Simplicissimus* (Independent Opera); *Insignificance* (Theatre Clwyd); Kommilitonen! (Welsh National Youth Opera / Opera Ieuenctid Cenedlaethol Cymru).

Assistant Director: Duncan Hallis

Duncan is a Director and Theatre-Maker, based in South Wales. He is Artistic Director of Big Loop, for whom he has Directed, Written and Performed.

As Theatre Director: *Cheer* (Big Loop/The Other Room); *Flours* (Big Loop); *Moirai* (Big Loop); *By Order Of* (Bert&Ernie/Depot – also writer); *The Birthday Party* (Just Talk/Studio Theatre).

As Film Director: *Random Shuffle* (It's My Shout/BBC/S4C)

As Theatre Performer: *The Ramshackles Brilliant Adventure* (Flossy and Boo – also deviser); *Extinct* (Yello Brick); *Hart to Heart* (Desperate Men – also deviser); *A Christmas Eve Party* (Big Loop – also deviser); *Flowers* (Big Loop – also writer); *Romeo & Juliet* (Sherman Cymru); *Punk Rock* (Just Talk); *Hay Fever* (Studio Theatre Salisbury); *My Boy Jack* (Studio Theatre Salisbury).

Other Collaborators Include: Stammermouth, Chippy Lane Productions, Difficult|Stage, Fio, Smut Slam International, Spilt Milk.

Matthew Bulgo

AMERICAN NIGHTMARE

OBERON BOOKS
LONDON

WWW.OBERONBOOKS.COM

First published in 2019 by Oberon Books Ltd
521 Caledonian Road, London N7 9RH
Tel: +44 (0) 20 7607 3637 / Fax: +44 (0) 20 7607 3629
e-mail: info@oberonbooks.com
www.oberonbooks.com

PB ISBN: 9781786829726
E ISBN: 9781786829719

Printed and bound by 4EDGE Limited, Hockley, Essex, UK.

Visit www.oberonbooks.com to read more about all our books and to buy them. You will
also find features, author interviews and news of any author events, and you can sign up
for e-newsletters and be the first to hear about our new releases.

Printed on FSC® accredited paper

10 9 8 7 6 5 4 3 2 1

Characters

CLARA, late twenties/early thirties

GREG, mid-thirties

DARIA, early twenties

ELWOOD, mid-twenties

THE PROGRAM

All of the characters are American except for Greg who is British

The character of THE PROGRAM could be played by an actor or a chorus but could just as well be represented through voiceover, multiple voices, video, projected text or any other way that the director sees fit

– indicates an interruption, either one character interrupting another or a character interrupting themselves

… indicates a trailing off

/ indicates a point of interruption resulting in overlapping dialogue

// indicates a second point of interruption, and /// a third, again resulting in overlapping dialogue

( ) words in brackets are not spoken and have been included for the sake of clarity

WHERE: America

WHEN: A future

silence, darkness

then chaos

light and dark compete for dominance

out of this…

night

a sky-line restaurant – sleek, opulent, tasteful, minimal

GREG: This place.

CLARA: You like?

GREG: I mean, wow.

CLARA: I know right?

GREG: That view.

CLARA: The best.

GREG: I was in the lift so long I thought I was going to get a nosebleed.

CLARA: Huh, that's good.

GREG: Seriously.

CLARA: We don't settle for anything less.

GREG: It's –

CLARA: It's the best is what it is.

GREG: It sure is.

    beat

CLARA: Can't lie: had to pull a few strings.

GREG: I bet.

CLARA: Not *that* many.

And besides, we like to look after our guests.

Speaking of which: eat what you want, drink 'til it comes out of your ears. Goes without saying but this is on us.

GREG: I have to admit, I've never really run with the whole out-of-hours, wining and dining thing, it's never really gelled with me truth be told –

CLARA: Hey –

GREG: Until now that is –

CLARA: I won't have a word said against it –

GREG: But this, a guy could get used to this –

CLARA: *'deals don't get made between 9 and 5, deals get made between dinner and dessert'.*

GREG: I like that.

> *beat*

CLARA: So you found us okay?

GREG: Driver knew just where to head. There was some sort of…a march going on. We had to take a detour, drive round the thing, streets were full, but your man seemed to know another way.

CLARA: Urgh. You're never more than ten yards away from someone protesting about something, am-I-right?

GREG: Right.

CLARA: 'specially right now. Lot of unhappy people. Not just here but all over. *You* know this. Things are broke.

GREG: You're right.

CLARA: That's the truth of the matter: things are broke. And when things are broke they need fixing.

GREG: Couldn't agree more.

CLARA: It's chaos out there.

> *beat*

Not that I'm complaining. Lotta profit in chaos.

> *beat*

Anyways, 'at's one of the benefits of being right the way up here.

GREG: What's that?

CLARA: You can't hear them screaming right the way down there.

she smiles, he does too but he's unsure

beat

Flight?

GREG: Flight was good.

CLARA: And the hotel? I trust we haven't asked you to slum it.

GREG: Are you kidding?

CLARA: You ought to try one of the rooms here sometime. You haven't lived until you've felt that sort of thread count against your skin.

GREG: Wow...

CLARA: Too much information?

GREG: No, no, it's –

CLARA: I don't care, it's true.

So, the hotel?

GREG: Yes, dropped the wife and kids off and they seemed happy enough! That was a nice touch by the way.

CLARA: Least we could do.

GREG: They don't get to travel with me all that often. They'll do a bit of sightseeing tomorrow while I fit in a couple of other meetings then we fly down to Philadelphia for a long weekend.

CLARA: Philadelphia.

GREG: My eldest, he's a total history nut. If we came all this way and we didn't go see the Liberty Bell I don't think he'd ever forgive me!

CLARA: Cute.

GREG: Isn't it?

beat

he scans the room, she observes him

GREG: Huh.

CLARA: What is it? Something / wrong?

GREG: No, it's nothing, / it's –

CLARA: What, what is / it?

GREG: Nothing, honestly –

CLARA: Please.

beat

GREG: I suppose I sort of feel…under-dressed!

CLARA: You are.

GREG: What?

CLARA: But we don't judge here.

GREG: Really?!

CLARA: Your suit, can I be honest, it does the job but it doesn't leave a lasting impression.

beat

(suddenly laughing) Your face, I'm playing with you. Most of the folks in this room have far bigger fish to fry, they're not gonna go getting themselves worked up over someone's sartorial choices.

GREG: Well, that's a relief!

CLARA: But next time, little bit of advice, I'd think of something a little more high-end.

4

beat

I'm joking! Relax.

GREG: Wow.

they laugh

Well at least one of us made an effort, right?

CLARA: Sorry?

GREG: You. I mean, you look – I don't know, can a guy say that these days?

CLARA: I don't know, you didn't say anything.

GREG: I was going to, I guess, compliment you, on your –

CLARA: Oh, well, thank you kindly.

GREG: I mean you do, you look –

CLARA: Formidable?

GREG: Ha. Well, that wasn't quite the word I was reaching for but –

CLARA: It wasn't?

GREG: Well…no.

CLARA: Then what was it?

GREG: I was going to say 'charming', I guess. 'Classy'.

CLARA: That works, 'classy' works, I guess.

GREG: But it wasn't what you were aiming for.

CLARA: No.

beat

GREG: Really?! You were *really* going for – ?

CLARA: Yes.

beat

GREG: Then yes, you do, you look formidable.

CLARA: Oh now you're just saying that.

GREG: No. Seriously. 'formidable'. '*Seriously* formidable'.

CLARA: Well, I'll drink to that.

raising her glass

I hope you don't mind but I took the liberty of ordering for us both.

GREG: Right… *(lifting his drink and peering at it)*

And what is one of these exactly?

CLARA: Dirty Martini.

GREG: Do I drink it or do I rub it in??

CLARA: Huh, that's good.

GREG: Ignore me, I'm just fooling around.

CLARA: *(he sips)* It's an acquired taste –

GREG: I hope so.

CLARA: You get used to it, you do.

GREG: *(sips)* So this is your tipple of choice? Dirty Martini.

CLARA: Dirtier the better.

Actually that's a lie, it's a delicate balance. The martini itself, it's crisp, like a streak of light – it's precise, it's incisive. Add the olive brine and you're in danger of spoiling all that. But if you want to strive for perfection you've got to take the risk that you're going to ruin everything, right?

GREG: Wow. I've never heard anyone talk like that about a drink before –

CLARA: Besides, they really know how to mix a good one here.

beat, he sips again

I can see if they have a beer if you'd rather. I'm sure
they'd be able to locate one.

GREG: No. No no, I'll stick with it.

CLARA: Perseverance. An admirable quality.

GREG: Got to try everything once right?

CLARA: You said it.

clink and drink

beat

GREG: So…

CLARA: So?

GREG: So do you want to tell me why I'm here?

CLARA: You shoot from the hip. Another admirable quality.

GREG: Sorry – the mysterious email, the furtive arrangements,
everything on the QT – I've got to admit, it's piqued my
interest, got me a little curious, so…

CLARA: 'So'. Again with the 'so' –

GREG: So, I thought we might get right down to it?

CLARA: What, no fore-play? But that's usually the best bit.

GREG: I…

CLARA: *(giggling)* I thought you'd've gotten your head 'round
my sense of humour by now.

GREG: You're very disarming, you know that.

CLARA: My God, you're blushing.

GREG: I am not!

CLARA: You are, you actually are.

GREG: Am I?

CLARA: Apologies. My line of work you've gotta find your
kicks any which way you can.

7

GREG: Right, and what is that exactly?

CLARA: Mmm?

GREG: Your line of work, what is it that you do?

CLARA: *(with a smile)* Oh. This-and-that. I keep out of trouble.

   beat

GREG: Do you want to be more specific?

CLARA: Mmm-not really, let's just say 'I get by'.

GREG: Then it seems you have me at a serious disadvantage.

CLARA: I guess I do, don't I.

GREG: And it looks like you're doing a hell of a lot more than just getting by.

CLARA: You're sharp, you know that?

   beat, she smiles, she goes to sip her drink, holding his gaze

GREG: Say who did you say you worked for again?

CLARA: I didn't.

GREG: Right…

   beat, she sips

   Wow, well that's an answer.

CLARA: Isn't it.

GREG: You bet.

CLARA: Nice try by the way.

GREG: Well, a guy's got to give it a shot.

CLARA: My people, they don't need to advertise.

GREG: That much is clear.

CLARA: We like to keep a low profile, what can I say.

   beat, putting down her drink

Let me put it this way: it would take a lot longer than one evening, over dinner, to explain the intricacies of the circles in which I move.

GREG: Right –

CLARA: It also wouldn't be good for your digestion.

GREG: I don't –

CLARA: What I do, Greg, is I do this: I talk.

beat

GREG: That's it?

CLARA: Uh-huh.

GREG: Just – talk?

CLARA: Pretty much, long-story-short.

I talk to people, people like you, at the behest of *other* people. I'm a conduit. I simplify matters.

GREG: Right…

she goes to drink, doesn't.

CLARA: I can't help but notice you're not drinking.

I can still ask about that beer, if you'd rather?

GREG: No, it's –

Old habit. Like to keep a clear head when it comes to business. I remember my father saying to me, when I was just starting out this was: *cut the deal first, drink to it after.* It's been my motto ever since.

CLARA: Sweet.

GREG: Is it?

CLARA: It is, it's real, I don't know, folksy, I guess.

beat, she plays with the olive in her drink

But sometimes it's worth coming at things a little differently. To alter one's perspective so to speak. *Nothing*

major ever got done without a bit of change, a bit of upheaval.
That's *my* motto.

GREG: Did your father say that?

CLARA: No. I did.

beat

Come on. Don't make me drink alone.

beat, he lifts his glass, he drinks

'at-a'boy.

she drinks

CLARA: First we eat.

Then I wanna show you something.

sound of chaos

light and dark compete for dominance

THE PROGRAM
all contact with the outside world is prohibited
all cell phones must be surrendered
all devices that transmit or receive are strictly forbidden
any contraband item discovered in your possession will be
destroyed and you will be permanently ejected from the
program
these precautions are for your own protection

–

each one a' you has a story
my momma's got cancer 'n' I can't pay for the treatment
my husband's too sick to work how'm I gonna put food on
the table
the repo man's taken everything I got, the bills, the debt, the
blah-di-fucking-blah
I could care less
you know what's good for you you'll keep that shit to yourself

show someone your weak spot and it's game over
let your story be the fuel in your gut that spurs you on
take a look at the person either side a' you
they ain't your friends they're your competition
empathy makes you weak

–

a period of decompression will commence upon arrival
from oh-nine-hundred-hours nothing comes in here and
nothing gets out

out of this…

a dorm room, empty but for a simple bed on either side of the space

DARIA lies on hers

ELWOOD sat, leant against the wall next to his

ELWOOD is a playing some kind of hand-held games console with ear-phones in

the sounds emanating from the ear-phones suggest the game is something violent and destructive

ELWOOD has a tranquil look on his face, his fingers moving smoothly and deftly over the various buttons

DARIA props herself up on her elbows and watches him

Eventually…

DARIA: Hey!

ELWOOD: …

DARIA: Said hey!

ELWOOD: …

DARIA: Hey, fella, hey –

ELWOOD: No talking.

DARIA: What?!

ELWOOD: Said no –

DARIA: Whatch'ya doing?

ELWOOD: No talking they said, didnj'ya hear them say that?

DARIA: Yeah, guess.

Mean they didn't really say that, not exactly but –

ELWOOD: But, right, they *implied* it so –

DARIA: Mmm-not *really* they didn't, 'f anything they kinda suggested it so…

beat

Just wondering what it was you got there is all.

beat

Said was just wondering what it was you –

ELWOOD: I heard you.

DARIA: So…

What is it? Thought phones were / contraband.

ELWOOD: 's not a phone.

DARIA: What?

ELWOOD: Said 'it's not a phone'.

DARIA: It ain't? Sure looks like a –

ELWOOD: 's a console –

DARIA: 's a what?

ELWOOD: Console, a games console.

DARIA: What, like a regular –

ELWOOD: Yeah, like a regular –

DARIA: What, like a video game?

ELWOOD: Y'right, whatever, a video game.

beat

DARIA: You're allowed those?

ELWOOD: Keeps my mind sharp.

DARIA: Said you allowed one a' –

ELWOOD: Got one, ain't I?

DARIA: Shit, 'f I knew I woulda brought me one of those things. Something to do I guess…Thought, I dunno, thought there'd be more stuff to do, like activities or whatnot, you know, when we weren't –

ELWOOD: Think this is? Some sorta summer camp?

DARIA: Well, no –

ELWOOD: 's 'at what you think this is?

DARIA: Know it ain't that but –

ELWOOD: Pfffff.

beat

DARIA: 's at supposed to mean?

ELWOOD shakes his head

DARIA: Hey, I said what's that supposed to mean?

ELWOOD plays his game

DARIA chuckles

silence

DARIA: So, wha's all 'at about?

ELWOOD: *(Pausing his game.)* What's what about?

DARIA: No cell phones, no television, what's with all that?

ELWOOD: Wanna keep us focused. 's my guess.

DARIA: You guess or you know?

ELWOOD: Neither, just supposing, way I see it they don't want nothing distracting us.

DARIA: Distracting us from / what?

ELWOOD: From whatever it is they want us to do, Genius.

DARIA: Which is / what?

ELWOOD: You ask too many questions, you know that?

beat, ELWOOD commences his game and cranks up the volume

DARIA lifts her top up and plays with her belly, she chuckles, she jiggles her belly

DARIA: Hell, I ain't eaten like that in I don't know how long.

ELWOOD: *(pulling one ear-phone out but continuing with the game)* You say something?

DARIA: Nothing, I was just –

Just making conversation is all.

Said I ain't eaten like that in forever.

ELWOOD: Yeah?

DARIA: Years, must be.

ELWOOD: Yeah.

DARIA: Feels good to get a hot meal inside-a-me, you know –

ELWOOD: Yeah…

DARIA: My gut didn't know what hit it.

ELWOOD: Oh yeah?

DARIA: Yeah…

ELWOOD: Right…

beat

DARIA: Wow, chatty sort a' guy, ain't you?

ELWOOD gives her a death stare whilst killing something significant on his game, there's a little fanfare

he pulls the earphones out, coils the wire around the game methodically

he hoists himself up onto the bed and puts the console under the end of his pillow

ELWOOD: Well, wouldn't go getting used to it 'f I were you.

DARIA: Used to what?

ELWOOD: The food

DARIA: Oh yeah, why's 'at

ELWOOD: Just wouldn't.

DARIA: 's 'at supposed to mean?

ELWOOD: What do you think it means, saying don't get used to it.

beat

DARIA: So, what…you been here before or something…

beat, ELWOOD gives her a glance but doesn't give her an answer either way

's your name, anyway?

beat

I'm Daria so…

So, what am I supposed to call you?

ELWOOD: How's about you don't call me nothing.

DARIA chuckles

DARIA: Okay!

God, you got a real endearing personality, you know that, say anyone ever told you that?

beat, she looks at him, fascinated

Could just give you a nickname, I guess.

Yeah, could just do that.

Prolly get annoying after a while though.

For you, I mean –

ELWOOD: Elwood! Just call me Elwood *(under his breath)* for Pete sake…

15

beat

DARIA: Call you that 'cause 'at's your name or call you that
'cause –

ELWOOD: It's my name, alright!

DARIA: Okay!

(sort of to herself) Elwood…El…wood.

Cool name, bro.

ELWOOD: Well, thanks.

DARIA: What?

ELWOOD: For the vote of confidence.

DARIA: You're so very welcome.

beat, she can't resist poking the bear

So what's your story, Elwood?

ELWOOD: D'in you hear what they said?

DARIA: What?

ELWOOD: Were you even listening?

DARIA: Sure I was, sure I heard.

ELWOOD: Well then.

DARIA: Hell, they was prolly just saying that for effect.

ELWOOD: You think?

DARIA: Sure, that was prolly all for effect and what-not.

ELWOOD: Okay –

DARIA: Don't you think?

ELWOOD: Sure, yeah, whatever you say, since you seem to
know so much.

DARIA: I'm just making conversation is all, I ain't looking for
a 'deep-and-meaningful' here, just, like, your hometown,
what's your hometown?

Come on, where you from?

Me, I'm from Topeka. Topeka, Kansas. You prolly already know that, so…

So where you from for chrissakes?

ELWOOD: I ain't your friend.

DARIA: Say again?

ELWOOD: Said I ain't your friend.

DARIA: Okay, cowboy –

ELWOOD: Sooner you get that idea into that head of yours the better.

DARIA: Okay –

ELWOOD: 'Less we know about each other – '

DARIA: You're something else –

ELWOOD: I'n't that what they said?

DARIA: You know that?

ELWOOD: That is what they said, isn't it?

DARIA: I heard what they said, I was just –

ELWOOD: What, you were just what?

    beat

DARIA: Interested is all, just shooting the crap, didn't mean nothing by it.

ELWOOD: Yeah, well –

DARIA: Just curious why you was here is all –

ELWOOD: Same reason as everyone else.

    beat

DARIA: Fair comment.

ELWOOD: Y'it is.

    he gets back on his bed

silence

DARIA: Well, I ain't got nothing to hide. Me, I tell you what, I am sick of dumpster diving, I gotta get me a change and I don't care how it happens. Hell, I been so low-down for so long, there's but only one direction I can go in and that's up!

DARIA chuckles

Sick a' stealing. sick a' living hand to mouth.

Mean, I ain't proud – and I don't go around telling everybody this – but I've sucked dick for a dollar, / I'm serious.

ELWOOD: Will you –

DARIA: Mean I didn't go making no habit out of it / or nothing, it was just like a bunch of times // like a coupla times sort of /// thing –

ELWOOD: / Hey.

// Hey! You –

/// You know what, I don't wanna hear it.

DARIA: What?

ELWOOD: Said I don't wanna know.

DARIA: Okay!

DARIA chuckles

beat

DARIA picks at something on her wrist then holds it up showing a small scar

DARIA: Okay so this ain't a personal question so you can't go getting mad and all but what's with these things they shoved in our wrists?

ELWOOD: 'f I tell you do you promise to quit flappin' your gums and shut the hell up?

DARIA: *(with a cheeky grin)* Ain't no point in making promises I can't keep now, is there?

ELWOOD: …

So's they can keep an eye on us, our vitals. Whiles we're sleeping. Whiles we're awake too, but mainly whiles we're sleeping.

DARIA: Vitals?

ELWOOD: Heart-rate, blood pressure, bunch a' other stuff. *(pointing to a light embedded in the wall above her bed)* Light's green you're fine. Turns orange, 'at means your getting het up. You don't wanna be there too long.

DARIA: You serious?

ELWOOD: They wanna know you fit the bill.

DARIA: Fit the bill how?

ELWOOD shrugs off her enquiry

(inspecting her wrist) For real? That's what these are for –

ELWOOD: *(with a wry smile)* No, I'm just entertaining myself, making shit up.

DARIA is unsure how to take this

DARIA: Shit, thought it was prolly GPS or something, so's they could keep tabs on us –

ELWOOD: *(lying back on his bed)* Prolly that too, how should I know –

DARIA: God damn!

ELWOOD stares at the ceiling

DARIA gets up and starts doing jumping jacks

After a few…

ELWOOD: *(propping himself up)* Hell you doing?

DARIA: Testing it.

ELWOOD: What for?!

DARIA: I'm testing it out.

ELWOOD: You think I'm fucking with you?

DARIA: How do I know? Could be for all I –

Light turns orange and a beep is emitted

I'll be damned!

she inspects her wrist with fascination, she chuckles to herself, gets her breath back, the light eventually turns back to green

ELWOOD: Turns red, you should be really worried

DARIA: Oh yeah, why's 'at?

ELWOOD: 'at means your dead.

DARIA: *(friendly)* Fuck off!

ELWOOD shrugs as if it say 'maybe I'm lying, maybe I'm not' then lies back down, closing his eyes

beat

she gets an idea, she creeps along the wall closer to his bed, crouching down next to him and scares ELWOOD by making a loud noise, he jumps, his light goes orange briefly

ELWOOD: The hell you playing 'at.

DARIA: *(laughing)* You just 'bout shit your pants.

ELWOOD: Said what the hell you –

DARIA: *(still laughing)* I'm just horsing.

ELWOOD: Fffff…

beat, DARIA's chuckle dies down

DARIA: Say you been here before, ain't you?

ELWOOD: Did I say that?

DARIA: Right though, ain't I?

ELWOOD: Didn't say that though, did I?

DARIA: But you have though, ain't you?

ELWOOD: Makes you think that –

DARIA: Just what you said, way you said it. 'don't get used to it'. Ain't that what you said? That *is* what you said, ain't it? Then about the chips in our wrists 'n' all. 'cause see that says to me you seem to know how things roll around here.

ELWOOD: Are you still talking?

DARIA: See 'at's what I think.

ELWOOD: 's that right?

DARIA: Reckon on it.

ELWOOD: Regular little Kojak, ain't you.

DARIA: Well, I'm right, ain't I?

ELWOOD: Well, you're wrong.

DARIA: Okay so how comes you know so much?

    beat

ELWOOD: *(sitting up)* I know a guy. On the inside. Worked similar projects, this was before, when this was still a military compound, but nothing like this. He said this one's new, this one's different. His words not mine.

DARIA: Different how?

ELWOOD: Bigger 'n before. Plus we ain't grunts are we. We're just regular Joes. Whatever it is – and I don't know – but said his folks are feeling real twitchy 'bout it. Everything being kept on the down-low.

DARIA: 'n' what else he say?

ELWOOD: *(with a hint of a smile)* 's all I know

    beat

DARIA: You know what we're doing here?

You know what it is we signed up for?

Well, do you?

he lies back against the wall and begins putting his earphones in

ELWOOD: *(with a grin)* I dunno. Guess we'll have to wait 'n' see.

ELWOOD resumes playing his game

sound of chaos

light and dark compete for dominance

out of this...

the restaurant

food has come and the last remnants remain on their plates, drinks have been freshened up, a tablet computer sits in the centre of the table

CLARA: A project.

A *construction* project.

Let's call it a '*major* construction project' which is why...I am talking to you. The talent.

GREG: Okay –

CLARA: You have the expertise...

GREG: Right.

CLARA: And we have...well, I suppose you could call it the 'testicular fortitude'.

GREG: The what – ?

CLARA: The balls, we have the balls.

she smiles, he sort of smiles and laughs not quite understanding her

GREG: Okay...

CLARA: Okay.

she swipes the tablet and nudges it toward him

Tell me what you see.

beat, he looks at it

GREG: I see –

I don't know –

I guess I see / a

CLARA: You know what? I'm going to stop you right there. For two reasons. First off, you should know this is time sensitive. Second of all, you need to know this is going to be huge. And you know what, now that I'm getting into my stride, I guess there's a third reason, and that's that I like you, and *because* I like you, I want you to have in on this.

GREG: You like me? We've only just met.

CLARA: I am a *very* good judge of character.

beat

GREG: Okay…

CLARA: So I'm just going to go right ahead and tell you what this is, if that's…?

GREG: Okay.

beat

CLARA: This is an opportunity.

beat

GREG: To do what?

CLARA: Whatever we want.

beat, she gives him a strange smile, she lifts her glass, he looks down at the screen, he inspects it

GREG: Wait. This scale. Something's got to be amiss here –

CLARA: I don't think so.

GREG: Has to be.

CLARA: Our people know what they're doing.

GREG: No, this has gotta be a mistake.

CLARA: We don't make mistakes.

GREG: But this has to be a footprint the size of, I don't know, the size of –

CLARA: …

GREG: A city?

CLARA shrugs as if to say 'kinda'

Are we talking about building a city?

CLARA: We're talking about it…

GREG: 'cause that's…I design museums, civic buildings, we build strip malls, we don't build – this is a little out of our league.

CLARA: Is it?

GREG: Something of this scale? We don't have the resources, the personnel to…not remotely, I mean, this would be bigger than anything we've ever –

CLARA: Do you know you're sweating?

beat

(breezily, shutting down the table and placing it in her bag) You know what, I'm gonna walk this back –

GREG: I'm sorry –

CLARA: It's fine –

GREG: Just thought –

CLARA: Honestly, it's –

GREG: Best to be upfront –

CLARA: Sure –

GREG: Say it like it is –

CLARA: I hear you –

GREG: I mean –

CLARA: Really.

GREG: Save everybody's time because –

CLARA: Listen, you know what: mea culpa. I must've been under some sorta misconception.

GREG: How so?

CLARA: I dunno, I guess I thought we had a common interest.

GREG: That being?

CLARA: Serious Business.

GREG: We do, I do, but like I said –

CLARA: Right, you said.

beat

GREG: Well this is (awkward) –

CLARA: It is…

beat

Can I ask you a question?

GREG: O-kay…

CLARA: There's no need to be nervous.

GREG: I'm not.

CLARA: Ha. Okay.

GREG: I'm / not.

CLARA: It's something I ask everyone I'm interested in doing business with. The response they give, it can be very telling.

GREG: Okay…

CLARA: Are you ready?

GREG: Sure…

beat

CLARA: Do you want to be respected? Or do you want to be envied?

beat

GREG: I don't know what you –

CLARA: I mean, in general, in life. Do you want people, when they think of you, to feel respect or do you want them to feel envy?

GREG: I've never really –

CLARA: Respect, envy. It's a binary question, Greg.

pause

GREG: I guess…respect – ?

CLARA: And that is your problem right there. You have too much substance. You think substance gets you places. I have news for you. Substance doesn't get you anywhere these days! You think substance gets you a penthouse on 5th overlooking the park? Do you think I paid for these teeth – with substance? Do you *honestly* think substance buys you a suit like this? These shoes? These shoes probably cost more than you pull down in a month by the way – I'm not kidding – probably two.

beat

Don't you ever think about having that sort of money?

GREG: Maybe.

CLARA: 'maybe'?

GREG: Well, I guess it would be nice.

CLARA: 'Nice'? *(with a laugh)* You crack me up. Who says 'nice' these days, Greg?

GREG: I'm sorry – I just meant –

CLARA: 'Want – to be – envied'.

Anything else: loser-mentality.

I don't mean to demean you by saying that. But it's true.
It is.

she takes a sip of her drink

an awkward beat

Listen. Can I tell you a story? I want to tell you a story.

sound of chaos

light and dark compete for dominance

we see DARIA and ELWOOD doing intense circuit training throughout this text

THE PROGRAM

decompression is done with

this is where the easy ride ends and the hard work begins

congratulations on making it this far

how far not very fuckin' far at all but congratulations all the
same

enjoy those words because those are the last words of
kindness that will pass through these lips

I am not here to give you an easy ride

I am not your councillor

I am not your mother

and I am certainly not your friend

I am here to get the job done

I am here to push you, to squeeze you for everything you've
got

I am here to chew you up and shit you out and that is exactly
what I am gonna do

out of this...

the dorm-room

ELWOOD sat on his bunk, DARIA bent over with hands on knees

they are out-of-breath, sweat patches on their clothes, moisture drips from their noses on to the floor

27

she's almost sick but there's nothing to come up

still out of breath…

DARIA: The fuck *was* that – ? They tryna kill us – ? 's 'at what they're after doing – ? 'cause if it is, if that's what they're – ? Yeah, I ain't really down with that –

'f I wanted to go to gym class I woulda stayed in fucking high school –

(beating the door) Hey! You listening? I did not sign up for this *shit!*

ELWOOD: *(under-his-breath)* 'cept you did.

DARIA: What?

ELWOOD: You wanna sit down.

DARIA: What for?

ELWOOD: Uh, you seem pretty agitated, it might help if you –

DARIA: I'll do what the hell I like.

ELWOOD: If you sat down.

DARIA: Been barked at all morning –

ELWOOD: Just sit down –

DARIA: Don't need you joining in –

ELWOOD: Fine, stand up, do what you like, fuck do I care, but if you're as wiped as you say you are, why don't you quit yelling at that wall, 'cause I don't think it's helping you any, and it certainly ain't helping me neither.

DARIA: They can't do this.

ELWOOD: Well…they can, they *are.*

DARIA: Someone's gotta complain 'bout this, someone's gotta kick up a stink.

ELWOOD: 'Complain'?

DARIA: Yeah –

ELWOOD: Are you for real?

DARIA: Fuck yeah I'm for real!

ELWOOD: They can do what the hell they like. *You signed up for this remember.*

DARIA: I signed up, right, but I'll be damned if I signed up for *this*, I'll be damned if I signed up to be treated like some fuck'n animal.

ELWOOD: Fine, go 'head.

DARIA: What?

ELWOOD: Go tell 'em.

DARIA: You think I won't?

ELWOOD: Nah, I think you're *actually* dumb enough to go do it. What exactly you think they'll do? Think they're gonna give you a hug? Hug-it-out, is that it? Think they'll give you a back rub? They're gonna laugh in your face and ship you out of here faster'n shit through a goose –

DARIA: *(lifting her food)* And they expect us to do *that*…they expect us to function on *this!*

This!!

she hurls her mess-tin at the wall, what little food is in it spills out

Ain't even food!

(clocking ELWOOD's mess tin and its contents) Hey, you got more 'n me.

ELWOOD: Well, you ain't got nothing now but okay I take your point –

DARIA: How you got more 'n me?

ELWOOD: 'cause I scored better 'n you, what d'you think?!

DARIA: Are you kidding me?

ELWOOD: Eyes on the prize!

DARIA: You cannot be serious.

ELWOOD: Hey, they're doing you a favour. Tomorrow you'll find an extra gear.

DARIA: And how do you figure that one out?

ELWOOD: 'Hunger focuses the mind'

beat

DARIA: What you say?

ELWOOD: Said –

DARIA: 'cause I think my ears are hearing things –

ELWOOD: Hunger –

DARIA: Things that ain't –

ELWOOD: It focuses the mind –

DARIA: Y'I thought 'at's what you / said –

ELWOOD: So why ask –

DARIA: They brainwashed you already?

ELWOOD: 's true.

DARIA: Oh boy!

ELWOOD: Scientific fact.

DARIA: You gonna get a t-shirt with that on before you check out of here?

ELWOOD: Laugh all you like, 's true. You would't know that though, wanna know why?

DARIA: Oh, why's 'at?

ELWOOD: 'cause you're weak is why.

DARIA: Wow, they got inside your head already, they have, haven't they?

ELWOOD: Scientific.

DARIA: I don't care if the angel Gabriel came down from on high and hand delivered it on a stone fucking –

ELWOOD: Ha.

DARIA: And never mind 'bout the portions, portions is another story, *it ain't even / food.*

ELWOOD: Okay.

DARIA: Don't fucking 'okay' me, Elwood. Don't fucking –

ELWOOD: *(with a smirk)* Shit, you can be awful mean when you're hungry, you know that.

DARIA: Screw you, Elwood.

ELWOOD: Aww, you didn't mean that did you, that really hurt.

she gives his bed an almighty kick, he laughs to himself

beat

ELWOOD: Hate to say I told you so.

DARIA: You wanna shut the hell up.

ELWOOD: Warned you, di'n I, not to get used to it –

DARIA: Yeah, you called it, alright –

ELWOOD: Did say that, di'n I?

DARIA: Alright already.

ELWOOD: Want my advice?

DARIA: Jesus, Elwood.

ELWOOD: You want it or not?

DARIA: I got a choice?

ELWOOD: Save your breath.

DARIA: 's 'at it?

ELWOOD: Save it 'cause you're gonna need it.

DARIA: 's 'at right?

31

ELWOOD: You bet. 'f you're serious about staying here you are.

DARIA: Give me a break will you –

ELWOOD: Got more a' the same this afternoon ain't we, you heard what they said –

DARIA: I heard –

ELWOOD: So –

DARIA: I heard, okay –

ELWOOD: But mainly, *mainly*, I'm telling you all this 'cause you're giving me a real doozie of a migraine if you really wanna know so –

DARIA: Yeah well maybe I ain't, maybe I ain't gonna need it 'cause maybe I am done with this, *I am done*, you hear me.

ELWOOD laughs

DARIA: Hell is wrong with you?

ELWOOD: Me, nothing.

DARIA: What?

ELWOOD: Nothing, just…

Can't lie, knew you wouldn't last long when the real work started but day one? Not even. Day *zero?* Woo, that really is something.

So what now? Back out there, back to the day job? Sucky-sucky for a buck a pop?

DARIA: Rrrrrrrgh.

she spears him and pins him down on the bed, her forearm across his throat

ELWOOD: Ah gee, I ain't got inside your head now, have I? Bet you wish you hadn't been so loose with those lips of yours now, no pun intended.

she applies more pressure

Go on then, girl!

beat

she gives him one last shove with her forearm before releasing him, he chuckles

You got juice, don't you. I'll give you that much.

Starting to make sense now? Why you don't tell no one nothing round here?

DARIA: You still talking?

ELWOOD: Yeah, I'm still talking.

DARIA: Go fuck yourself.

ELWOOD: What? I was just calling it. Knew you wouldn't last.

DARIA: Oh yeah?

ELWOOD: Y'I'd a' put money on it. Know why? 'cause you don't get it.

DARIA: Get it, what's to get?

ELWOOD: You want an easy ride, you want something for nothing. World don't work like that no more. World ain't worked like that for a very long time.

DARIA: No shit.

ELWOOD: You of all people should know that.

he mimes sucking a penis

DARIA: …

I came in here 'cause I was near-starvin' out there. Hunger din't help me out there any and it ain't helping in here neither.

ELWOOD: 'cept there's a difference ain't there? In here there's an incentive. Light at the end of the tunnel. 'd you forgotten about that?

DARIA: …

ELWOOD: Nothing comes for free. Gotta work for it.

Rather be in here than out there, tell you that for nothing.

beat

So walk.

DARIA: What?

ELWOOD: Walk. Can't hack it, then walk, fuck do I care. Fact is you'd be one less person in my way.

DARIA: I ain't –

I didn't say I was thinking a' –

ELWOOD: Kinda did. 'I'm done'. Ain't that what you said? Yeah, 'I'm done'. See 'at sorta sounds like –

DARIA: Yeah, well, those were just words –

ELWOOD: Oh, okay –

DARIA: They could mean anything –

ELWOOD: So what did you mean?

DARIA: Di'n't actually say –

ELWOOD: Di'n't have to.

beat

Hell, do what you want. Stay and suck it up or get the hell out of here. Really don't matter to me.

DARIA: All I'm saying's, they di'n't say nothing about no fitness test. Di'n't say I was gonna have to do some fucking decathlon just to –

ELWOOD: They didn't say nothing 'bout nothing.

DARIA: …

Yeah…

beat

ELWOOD: Anyways, it ain't about fitness.

DARIA: What?

ELWOOD: It ain't about fitness –

DARIA: Coulda fooled me.

ELWOOD: They don't give a shit about that –

DARIA: So what, they're just doing this, what, for kicks, to humiliate us or –

ELWOOD: No –

DARIA: 's 'at it?

ELWOOD: Ain't about that –

DARIA: Certainly seems that way –

ELWOOD: Think what you want –

DARIA: So what then, what is it about?

beat

ELWOOD: Obedience, Genius.

's about your ability to listen to orders 'n' 'en carry 'em out.

They could give two shits 'bout how fit you are.

They want *unparalleled obedience.* That no matter what they ask you to do, no matter how much fuckin' pain you're in – physical, psychological or otherwise – that you're gonna do it, no pushback, no questions asked. A straight line, no deviation. They don't even want you to consider the question – do-I-don't-I, do-I-don't-I – they just want you to act…and judging by how much you're whining like a bitch on day one, sorry day *zero*, yeah, I prolly wouldn't go getting comfortable 'f I were you…

'cause if you can't drag yourself through this ain't no way you're gonna stomach what's to come.

DARIA: And what's that?

beat, ELWOOD smirks

ELWOOD: You know what, I wouldn't worry about it.

DARIA: Why not?

ELWOOD: Just, got a feeling you ain't gonna make it that far.

DARIA: So then tell me.

beat

ELWOOD: You're gonna do some stuff here that's gonna stick with you. Stuff that'll give you nightmares. That's why the doohickies.

he indicates the chip in his wrist

DARIA: How bad can it be?

ELWOOD shrugs knowingly

beat

ELWOOD: Physical stuff, they won't keep that up for more 'n a week. Breaking us in is all. Gotta tell the wheat from the chaff somehow. End of the week they'll be shipping hundreds outta here, thousands prolly. Want a chance of making the cut, you gotta least last 'til then.

DARIA: Why should I believe you?

ELWOOD: Take it or leave it, no skin off my ass.

DARIA: And how come's you know all this anyway?

ELWOOD: I know a guy.

DARIA: Right…your guy.

beat, ELWOOD eats

ELWOOD: You could make the cut no sweat. You seen some a' these losers. Your problem is you don't want it enough.

DARIA: 'f you really don't give a shit about me, how comes you're telling me all this?

ELWOOD: *(grinning)* 'cause you ain't no threat to me.

ELWOOD gets up and looks at DARIA's food on the floor, nudging the mess tin with his foot

Gonna eat that? 'cause I'd prolly pick the dirt off of that 'f I were you.

DARIA: Oh yeah. Why's 'at?

ELWOOD: 'cause you won't be getting nothing else 'til this time tomorrow.

ELWOOD smiles, he gets comfortable on his bunk

beat

she moves toward the food, sits on the floor next to it and leans against the wall

she reaches for the food

sound of chaos

light and dark compete for dominance

out of this…

the restaurant, CLARA and GREG pick at the food left on their plates

CLARA: This was when I was a kid.

We'd spend June-through-August out at this summer house out in Mount Vernon, the 'rents and me.

Most days, I'd walk, down through the woods, explore, down to the creek and back.

One weekend, this one particular summer, we had family over to visit – aunts 'n' uncles, cousins, the whole circus.

So we walk down to the creek, two of the cousins and me, both boys, both a little older.

The day's scorching so we take our swimsuits, figure we can horse around in the water.

Anyway, we're out there splashing away when we feel eyes on us…and when we look back toward the tree-line there's this…dog, stood there, gawking at us.

We swim back, back to the shore, and it's this grey thing. I don't know all-that-much about dogs but it's a mutt I'd say. No collar, so we figure: stray, must be.

The thing skitters over to us – the skin's all thin, papery, fur's all matted – and it looks up at us with these big, stupid, old dog eyes, its tongue all hanging out and all, you know the way they do.

We threw sticks. Wasn't interested. Tried playing with it. Nothing doing. See, it wanted feeding, that's what it wanted, it wanted food.

So what we do, is we feed it some scraps, from our back-packs – 's the boys' idea – and when it's done, it looks up at me and it…licks my hand and that…

she shakes her head and smiles, almost imperceptibly.

Next day, we go back down there, the three of us, only this time we take some extra for the dog, case it's there again.

And it is, it's there waiting for us, so we feed it. And I couldn't quite put my finger on it at the time, but there was something about that…that fascinated me.

beat

Down by the water's edge we find a bit of old rope and we fashion a sort of leash, figure we'll take him walking with us, why not.

And he comes with us, no issue. You see, something had formed between us. A bond, I guess. We gave him what he wanted – just enough of it anyway – and he trusted us.

My cousins, they head back to the house, they're heading off that night you see, back to the city, but me, I keep on walking, me and the dog that is.

beat

We get back to the creek, later this is, and I let him go, figure he'll wander on off back to where he sleeps or whatever, and I start to walk back up through the woods toward the house…and it's the craziest thing but it follows me, not too close, but its there, like, ten yards behind me, and every time I turn around, it stops and stands there looking at me with those big, stupid, old dog eyes.

Eventually, I'm like okay, let's see how this plays out, and I just stand there, stare the thing out, 'who's going to blink first?', you know.

's not long before it hobbles on over and it sits there in front of me

(almost dreamily, to herself) 'at a boy.

Then what it does, is it licks at my hand, and that – yeah – like I said before – that just…

she shakes her head and smiles, almost imperceptibly

Thing musta followed me for a mile or more. Sure I don't need to tell you this, you're a bright guy, but it wanted me to provide. That's what it had come to expect from me during this fleeting relationship.

Thing is…I didn't have anything for it. And even if I did…I wasn't sure whether I wanted to give it.

beat

Daddy – he always hated dogs – never let me have one as a kid. My point being there was no way this dog was coming home with me. Father dearest would flip his wig to say the very least. So I take its leash, this rope we'd found, and what I do, is I loop it around this tree, and I leave it there.

beat, she sips at her drink leaving him hanging on

39

Next morning, my pa gets called back into the city for work, so we get set to head back to DC. Says it could be a week, could be more, who knows.

And I thought about that dog, sitting out there, tied to that tree…

And then I let that thought pass.

beat

Anyway, one week turns into two, two to three, three to four, and I sorta forget about my little doggy friend if I'm perfectly honest. He just sorta slips off the old radar. Until we get back that is. Then? Then I'm kinda curious, I guess. Curious how the little critter's doing out there, all tied up to that big ole tree.

beat

At first, I don't see it, thinking 'what the hell?'. When I get closer, I see it's lying there, it's just I couldn't see it what with all the plants 'n' weeds 'n'what-not that had sort of sprouted up around it.

It sort of opens it's eye, just the one – thing was still alive, just. Hadn't even chewed at the rope. Hadn't even thought to do that, the dumb dog.

Then I see – and I don't for the *life* of me know how it's done this, I have *no idea* – but the thing has clawed away at its own flank, chewed at its own tail. It must've – I don't know – dislocated something, *it must've*, otherwise how could it have even done that…

beat

a grin grows and blooms into a short, sharp giggle

God, it felt wrong but I couldn't help smiling. I guess because…I don't know, I guess I learned something truly profound at that moment. You could even say it was formative.

(as if quoting a proverb) A dog'll eat its own tail if it's hungry enough.

It will. I've seen it.

she has a fork full of food

I think of that dog often. *(nonchalantly)* It was looking for love I guess. Love, compassion, whatever, I don't know.

beat

(realising suddenly) I've never told anyone that.

beat

How was the Wagyu by the way? I find it sits a little heavy.

silence but the sound of CLARA's fork on plate

GREG: Wow, that's –

Did that –

Did that actually happen?

beat, smiles as if to say 'I guess you'll never know'

CLARA: *(suddenly)* Actually that's a total lie.

GREG: *(relieved)* Oh, that's –

CLARA: Yeah, I've told that story heaps of times. Don't know why I said that. Definitely happened though.

dabs her mouth with her napkin

GREG: Right.

How – how old were you?

CLARA: Five. Five or six. I don't remember.

GREG: Wow –

I –

I don't –

CLARA: What is it?

GREG: I…have no idea why you just told me that.

CLARA: I dunno, just a story, I thought we were just talking, weren't we?

GREG: Right but I…I just don't see what your point is –

CLARA: My point? Oh God, my point, let's see – neither do I. I guess I'm just grasping at something – you know that way you do – like it's in your peripherals but you just can't…

beat, thinks, shakes her head as if to say 'no, nothing'

I'm sure it'll become apparent.

beat

GREG: What did you do to it?

CLARA: I'm sorry?

GREG: What did you do?

CLARA: …?

GREG: I mean, did you set it free? Did you put it down? Is that what you did?

she smiles as if she hasn't heard any of the questions

CLARA: I forget.

GREG: What?

CLARA: I don't recall.

beat, GREG starts to laugh

GREG: Is this –

Is this one of your – you being humorous or whatever –

CLARA: No. It's definitely not that.

GREG: …

CLARA: I guess this is me trying to elucidate the difference between you and I.

GREG: I don't –

42

CLARA: Greg. Don't speak. Just listen.

GREG: …

CLARA: Good. That's good.

> *(reintroducing the tablet)* This is one of a number of similar projects. You are one of a number of people we're speaking to. But right now, I am talking to you.
>
> So why don't you take another look.
>
> *she swipes the tablet*
>
> *sound of chaos*
>
> *light and dark compete for dominance*
>
> *DARIA and ELWOOD take part in exercises to test their hand-eye coordination and reaction times*
>
> *the exercises accelerate, music is pumped into their ears*

THE PROGRAM

I have been doing this for a very long time and I'll be doing it for a very long time to come you wanna know why *because I am exceptional at what I do and because I do not accept bullshit*

follow my example and you'll go far but never as far as me because I will always be better than you
this is the attitude you must have anything less is loser-mentality

–

you will be charged with tasks that will challenge your physical and cognitive abilities
your ability to follow instructions both basic and complex
your scores will be displayed on the screen at the head of the room and will be refreshed every ten seconds
if you hit your targets you will advance
if you are the weakest runt in the litter you will not

end of each day the lowest scoring individual will be frog-
marched out of the compound and sent on their way you
think I'm joking I am not joking I will be the one frog-
marching you and I will take great pleasure in doing so
we do not have the time space or energy for deadwood
understood
I do not need to hear your answer because if you do not
understand you won't be here long

out of this…

the dorm-room

DARIA is lying on her back, covering her eyes with her hands

*ELWOOD is sitting upright on his bed playing his games console, his
fingers and eyes moving quicker than before as is the action of the game*

*There is some sort of 'game over' sound and he throws the console down
on the bed*

He presses his palms into his eyes

beat

He looks at DARIA and judging by her breathing thinks she's asleep

*ELWOOD proceeds to retrieve a small canister of pills that he has secreted
somewhere, removing it carefully in case the sound alerts DARIA*

*He removes one pill from the canister again being careful not to make
any noise*

He pops the pill into his mouth and dry-swallows it

*He is in the process of hiding the canister when DARIA opens her eyes
and clocks him*

DARIA: What *are* those?

    DARIA's voice startles him and he drops the canister

ELWOOD: *(as he retrieves it)* Thought you was sleeping.

DARIA: I was. Trying at least.

ELWOOD: So?

DARIA: Can't. Spots in front of my eyes.

ELWOOD: You should try for some shut-eye, prolly need it –

DARIA: Yeah, not happening.

ELWOOD: Suit yourself.

DARIA: Ears ringing too. They have to spout that shit into our heads? It ain't even music.

ELWOOD: 'Train hard, fight easy', ain't that what they said.

DARIA: 'fight'?

ELWOOD: What?

DARIA: It's a goddam arcade game.

ELWOOD: Right.

DARIA: Not even a *good* arcade game.

ELWOOD: Gets repetitive, don't it?

DARIA: Y'after six hours straight it does.

ELWOOD: Yeah.

DARIA: So what were those?

ELWOOD: What?

DARIA: You know what. I ain't blind, Elwood.

ELWOOD: Nothing.

DARIA: Sure didn't look like nothing. 'cause if those're aspirin, you need to gimme.

ELWOOD: …

DARIA: Seriously, the hell were those? *(advancing)* You want me to strip search you, 'cause I will.

ELWOOD: They ain't aspirin so –

DARIA: So then what?

ELWOOD: …

'Performance enhancing'.

beat

DARIA: What?!

ELWOOD: What I said.

DARIA: So like…

ELWOOD: Yep.

DARIA: Seriously?

ELWOOD: Oh yeah.

DARIA: You mean like –

ELWOOD: Right –

DARIA: In the sack?! Fuck d'you need *those* for?!

ELWOOD: No! Course not in the sack, are you high?

DARIA: So then what?

ELWOOD: Focus, for chrissakes, concentration!

One part military-grade speed, one part Ritalin, and then some shit that puts it all on slow release.

Better my concentration, better my scores. Better my scores, longer I'll be in here.

DARIA: The hell'd you get those?

ELWOOD: I know a guy.

DARIA: Right, your guy.

ELWOOD: 's 'at supposed to mean?

DARIA: Same guy, different guy?

ELWOOD: What?

DARIA: Nothing. Just seem to know a lotta guys is all. Was wondering which one's dick you had to suck to get your mitts on those.

ELWOOD: You're the only cocksucker 'round here.

DARIA: Self-confessed but you're still in the closet.

ELWOOD: *(rearing up)* Fuck you!

DARIA: Woah there, stud. Just playing with you is all. Didn't mean nothing by it. Those things affect your mood too, your hormones 'n' what-not?

ELWOOD: Kiss my ass.

beat, as he backs down and turns away from her she makes a kissing sound

he turns and glares, she smiles

beat, he sits

DARIA: How many those things you got anyway?

ELWOOD: Enough.

DARIA: Enough to share?

ELWOOD: No way.

DARIA: Come on, how's about it?

ELWOOD: How's about what?

DARIA: Gimme one for chrissakes!

ELWOOD: Hell no, you crazy, this is my stash –

DARIA: Elwood, one.

ELWOOD: Every man for himself round here. The hell would I wanna help you for?

DARIA: One is what I'm asking for! Just want to see for myself, what it feels like, the buzz, 'at's all.

ELWOOD: *(negative)* Uh-uh.

DARIA: You've seen my scores.

ELWOOD: *(laughing)* Yeah!

DARIA: Yeah, so you know I ain't vying for nothing – just gimme one day where I don't totally embarrass myself on the scoreboard. 's all I'm asking.

ELWOOD: Leave it.

DARIA: Come on, Elwood, don't be such a freaking –

ELWOOD: No means no –

DARIA: You got enough of those things to last 'til the end of days, I just saw.

ELWOOD: Look: ain't no way I'm giving you one of these, are you out of your tiny mind, so just give it a rest will you.

beat

DARIA: A'right.

A'right, so what I gotta do to get me one?

ELWOOD: What do you have that I could possibly want?

DARIA: You want today's food allowance, you got it.

ELWOOD: I don't want your food, ain't nothing you got that I need, believe me, so just give it up.

he pops another pill

DARIA: Di'n you just pop one a' those?

ELWOOD: So I'm popping another one, what's it to you, you're not my ma.

beat, they settle

DARIA: You even allowed those things?

ELWOOD: You wanna know something: 'People who follow the rules almost always lose'.

DARIA: Well, are you?

ELWOOD: Listen: they'll turn a blind eye to anything that's gonna help them get the job done.

DARIA: …?

ELWOOD: You heard about Larson right? Big dude, end of the hallway?

DARIA: Heard there was something but I didn't hear what.

ELWOOD: Went ape-shit. Took his pull-up bar off of the doorframe and beat his room mates' brains out with it. While he was sleeping. And you've seen him. Guy that size. He's a fucking animal.

DARIA: Why'd he – ?

ELWOOD: Fuck should I know. Guy's taken so many steroids his balls have prolly damn near imploded. When the guards got there, he was stood there covered in this guy's blood. Said he couldn't stop laughing his ass off.

Now tell me something: what do you think's gonna happen to him?

DARIA: I think they're gonna kick him off the program.

ELWOOD: They'll prolly give the guy a freaking commendation. Prolly pinning a medal on his big, beefy chest right now.

DARIA: Why would they do that?

ELWOOD: You are seriously dumb as shit you know that.

He fits the bill. He's the sort of person they're looking for. He's willing to step on throats to get what he wants. When he did what he did, he was letting 'em know he's serious.

beat

's like I said. They're gonna turn a blind eye. They just want the job done.

beat

DARIA: What job?

beat, ELWOOD smirks

You keep saying that, what job, what are we doing here, Elwood?

ELWOOD's smirks turns into a laugh

ELWOOD: Shit, you really ain't figured this out yet have you?

DARIA: What's there to figure?

ELWOOD: What you been doing all day, Genius?

DARIA: You know what I've been doing all day / so why ask, same as // you –

ELWOOD: / So what?

//So then what?

DARIA: You know what – more fucking games, shoot this, swipe that, might as well be playing Donkey Kong.

ELWOOD: So?

DARIA: …

ELWOOD: They're priming us, dumb-ass.

DARIA: For what?

ELWOOD: The real thing.

silence

DARIA: Drones?

ELWOOD: Eureka. Somebody give this girl a cigar!

DARIA: Is that what this is, drones?

ELWOOD: Course fucking drones, are you retarded?

DARIA: You mean –

ELWOOD: You get dropped on your head as a kid or something?

DARIA: Like, *drones*?

ELWOOD: Not *like* drones, *drones*, actual –

DARIA: You know what I mean, *drone* drones.

ELWOOD: How many types a' drones are there / exactly?

DARIA: Stop fucking around, Elwood. Drones that like –

ELWOOD: What? Kill people?

DARIA: Yeah.

ELWOOD: Pfffff.

   beat

   What people?

ELWOOD: Who cares?

DARIA: What people, Elwood?

ELWOOD: (How) should I know?

DARIA: You seem to know everything else 'round here.

ELWOOD: Some rag-heads in some fucking country I couldn't find on a map if you paid me. 's it matter?

DARIA: Yes.

ELWOOD: Not to me it don't –

DARIA: You fucking serious?

ELWOOD: You bet.

   beat

DARIA: You think they were gonna mention that at some point?!

ELWOOD: What?

DARIA: Eight weeks we been here, said you think they were going to mention that –

ELWOOD: They'll mention it when they're good and ready. Wanna know you're up to the task first. They'll mention it when you're neck-deep.

DARIA: What's at supposed to mean?

ELWOOD: You don't see it, do you? They're shifting the goalposts every day, just a little, so small you don't even see it, but they are. They're seeing how far we're willing to go.

And why? 'cause they can. 'cause we got no choice in the matter. They're the ones feeding us, they're the ones putting a roof over our heads, flashing the bucks. 's an incentive. There's an incentive there. And as soon as there's an incentive in the equation, what you're willing to do, that ain't up to you no more, not really that's up to someone else. The ones calling the shots.

And they shift a little here, and they shift a little there, and before you know it, they'll have you eating out of their palms. You'll do whatever they want, anything they ask. Roll over, play dead, hell they'll have you licking your own balls if they feel like it.

And 'fore you know it, you're so far down the line that turning back? That ain't a option no more.

beat

Aww, what's the matter, feeling duped?

DARIA: Yeah, well, shouldn't I be?

ELWOOD: See, I knew what I was walking into, I've known since day one, and you know what, I'm cool with it. You? You feel duped, you feel cheated, and right now that smarts….but it'll pass. And once it has, you'll do those things, whatever they ask of you, you will, trust me. Know why? 'cause they got their grip on you. Might not feel it, but they have.

silence

Wow, 'f I knew that would shut you up I'd a' told you weeks ago.

DARIA: You're talking about all this like it's –

ELWOOD: Like it's what?

Listen to me: once you get outta here, only person that's gonna need to live with this is you. So box it up in your head, shove it somewhere you ain't gonna find it all 'at often, and get on with your life with some serious dough in your pockets.

DARIA: That easy, huh?

ELWOOD: That easy.

> What's the alternative, huh? Back out there, 'dumpster diving', ain't that what you called it. You want that life, you go for it.

> This is an opportunity. When was the last time you had one a' those? One like this? I'll tell you: never's the answer. Think about that.

> *beat*

> Anyway, ain't no point putting the cart before the horse now, is there. You ain't got that far yet.

> *beat*

DARIA: You…

ELWOOD: What?

DARIA: Nothing.

> *beat*

> You ever killed anyone, Elwood?

ELWOOD: Me?

DARIA: s'what I asked.

ELWOOD: …

DARIA: Well have you?

> *beat*

ELWOOD: No.

> But I could. Long as I din't have to look 'em in the eyes.

> *beat*

> You?

DARIA: Hell no.

ELWOOD: Course you ain't.

beat, opening the lid of his canister of pills

Well, you'd better start getting used to the idea.

closes the lid

'at makes you squeamish, there's the door.

he switches on his games console

sound of chaos

light and dark compete for dominance

out of this…

the restaurant

the tablet is sat on the table between them

GREG: I don't think you understand.

The things I said before. They still stand. A project of this scale – my company, we're not equipped, not remotely –

CLARA: Forget about manpower a minute, Greg. Forget about resources and finances and all those finicky little details, forget about *all that.* Say none of those things were an issue. What then?

GREG: But they are.

CLARA: I'm saying they're not.

GREG: From where I'm sitting, they /are –

CLARA: And I'm saying they're not.

GREG: Just like that?

CLARA: Just – like – that.

beat, GREG surrenders temporarily and surveils the map

GREG: Some context would be useful.

I still don't really know what I'm looking at.

I mean, where even is this?

beat, CLARA is inscrutable

Wait.

beat

Okay, wait.

beat

Is this –

beat

Is this…the Middle East? 'cause if it is –

CLARA: Middle East is a very big place.

GREG: So it *is* the Middle East?

CLARA: I was merely passing comment.

GREG: So is it the Middle East or isn't it?

CLARA: I couldn't possibly say.

GREG: Why not?

CLARA: Just can't.

GREG: Because that makes it sound like it probably is –

CLARA: There are things I can say at this stage and there are
things that I cannot.

beat, putting down the tablet

GREG: Okay, okay, okay, right, is this – is this whole – is this
a *government* kinda thing?

CLARA: 'Kinda thing'?

GREG: Because that's the sort of feeling I'm getting right now
–

CLARA: It is? Really?

GREG: Well, is it?

CLARA: No.

GREG: You know what I'm saying, don't you –

CLARA: Yes –

GREG: What I'm getting at –

CLARA: I think so –

GREG: I'm saying like a government...*military* kinda thing.

CLARA: Right.

GREG: So, is it?

beat

CLARA: Would it matter if it was?

beat

GREG: Mmm-yes. It would.

CLARA: Really?

GREG: Yeah, see that – that'd – yeah, no, that'd make me
   a little uncomfortable. To say the very least. I'm talking
   morally here. Yeah, I don't think I'd feel at all comfortable
   aligning my company with those sorts of...morally
   questionable –

CLARA: Right.

GREG: Yeah.

beat

CLARA: Would you be relieved, would things be back on the
   table, if I told you this was *not* in the Middle East?

GREG: Well, that'd be one thing but –

CLARA: We're not talking about the Middle East, Greg.

GREG: Right.

CLARA: This isn't the Middle East.

GREG: Yeah?

CLARA: It's not.

GREG: Okay –

CLARA: You think I'd lie to you?

GREG: No, no, I –

CLARA: I would not lie to you. 'cause I think trust is really important when it comes to a working relationship.

GREG: I do trust you, I do –

CLARA: I'm glad –

GREG: It's just that –

CLARA: And this isn't what you think it is. This isn't a government thing, this isn't a military thing, the military aren't remotely involved in this little project.

GREG: No?

CLARA: Not remotely. This goes way above all that. This is 'business'.

beat, she smiles, he smiles eventually

GREG: So if it's not the Middle East then –

CLARA: There he is. 'mr. Perseverance'. Sorry –

GREG: I just want to know what we're –

CLARA: Right now can't say.

GREG: Really?!

CLARA: Need to know basis. *Really.*

GREG: And I don't fit into that category?

CLARA: Not just yet you don't.

beat

Listen, you ever hear that phrase 'a place at the top table'?

GREG: I –

CLARA: Rhetorical question, Greg. No need to answer. See, there was a time I thought that was just something people said. A turn of phrase. Turns out it's an actual thing. *(indicating the room)* This is it. *This* is the top table. You could pull up a seat but right now you're dithering in the doorway.

All you *really* need to know, is once this breaks the market is going to be flooded with opportunities. *Flooded.* And this is your chance to come and sup on the cream whilst everyone else is fighting over the slops.

'a rising tide lifts all boats'. Question you need to ask yourself is do you wanna be in some dinghy, bailing water with your hat, paddling along with all the other no-hopers…or do you want to be aboard the Good Ship Prosperity?

pause

GREG: I'm sorry. I don't do business like this. I need to know what I'm walking into. And right now – if this is all you can give me – that's, for me, that's problematic. I'm sorry. It was really nice meeting you. Thank you, for your hospitality –

he half-stands

CLARA: Stop.

GREG: I'm sorry –

CLARA: Sit.

beat, he does

Greg. I really didn't want to resort to this, it always leaves me feeling a little grimy but…

reaches across and takes his napkin

Let me put this into a language that'll oil the wheels somewhat.

sound of chaos

light and dark compete for dominance

THE PROGRAM

you have all made it this far because you share a particular
set of attributes exceptional hand-eye coordination mental
aptitude and the ability to shout HELL YES when your moral
compass is yelling getthefuckoutofhere
we have seen your upper limits and now we wanna see how
much further you can go
we are going to push you
we will push you until you have *new* limits
until you are capable of things you never imagined possible
until you've given us every goddam thing you've got

out of this…

the dorm room, night

*there's a creaking noise and the sound of muffled music coming from
ELWOOD's side of the room*

DARIA: Elwood, the hell you doing over there?

> *beat*

> Hey! You wanna knock it off?

> *she puts a pillow over her head momentarily before springing up
> and moving to his side of the room*

> Will you shut the hell up, I'm tryna sleep over here!

> *she flicks the light on, ELWOOD's like a startled deer, he pulls his
> earphones out, his light flashes orange and beeps*

ELWOOD: Jesus! What are you, you scared the living –

DARIA: The hell you playing at, is there something wrong
with you –

> *beat*

> Wait a minute, were you –

ELWOOD: No, I wasn't, definitely not –

DARIA: Oh-my-God, Elwood, were you jerking off? 's'at what you were doing?

ELWOOD: Uh, no.

DARIA: Jesus, Elwood, least you could do is use the bathroom like a regular human being, fuck is wrong with you?

ELWOOD: I was not 'jerking off' as you so eloquently –

DARIA: Oh-my-god, you were, you were beating one out, I could hear you for chrissake –

ELWOOD: I was not, I was –

DARIA: No?

ELWOOD: No.

DARIA: *(noting the bump in the blanket)* Certainly looks that way.

ELWOOD: *(hiding the bump)* We get erections when we sleep, so's we don't you know –

DARIA: No I don't know.

ELWOOD: So's we don't piss the bed. Not that I've even got one anyway, but that is a fact, that is a scientific –

DARIA: You are so full a' horseshit –

ELWOOD: I was not 'beating one out', okay, or 'jerking off' or whatever you want to call it, so if you don't mind –

DARIA: Oh, I don't mind –

ELWOOD: I'd like to get some shut-eye –

DARIA: You ain't listening, said I don't mind.

ELWOOD: What

DARIA: I don't mind *at all.*

ELWOOD: …

DARIA: *(slowly advancing)* Fact is, it's sorta got me a little hot under the collar, 'f you really wanna know so.

ELWOOD: Wha's 'at supposed to –

DARIA: You know what I mean, Elwood. Got me feeling horny now and 'at's a fact.

ELWOOD: Will you quit fooling?

DARIA: I ain't fooling. Cooped up in a place like this, no ways to get your kicks, 's bound to get you a little worked up, ain't it.

ELWOOD: I told you, I wasn't and I ain't so –

DARIA: You sure about that?

she reaches under the blanket

ELWOOD: Hey.

DARIA: 'cause it certainly feels like you are. Or is it me. Is it me your pleased to see?

ELWOOD: What, what are you, you're touching my –

DARIA: I know what I'm doing –

ELWOOD: What –

DARIA: You don't have to tell me, Elwood –

ELWOOD: But –

DARIA: Shhh. 's okay. I can help you get rid of that, 'f you want?

she starts to masturbate him

There now, that ain't so bad is it, *(she spits into her palm and swaps hands)* fact that feels pretty good don't it.

ELWOOD: No, no, it's –

DARIA: Don't it feel good.

ELWOOD: No, I mean yeah, yeah it does, but it's – the monitor –

DARIA: *(giggling)* Oh, I get it, you want it soft don't you, soft and gentle, like that?

ELWOOD: Yeah, yeah, that's, oh boy

DARIA: Yeah, that feels good, don't it.

ELWOOD: I guess…

DARIA: Beats rubbing one out 'gainst the mattress, don't it?

ELWOOD: Oh yeah.

DARIA: Yeah it does, sure it does.

ELWOOD: Oh shit.

DARIA: Wow, you're wound pretty tight, ain't you.

ELWOOD: Yeah, oh, yeah.

DARIA: You gonna make it for me? Huh? You gonna make it for me?

ELWOOD: Oh, momma!

DARIA: Yeah, that's it.

he ejaculates, he takes a moment to get his breath back

he moves his head toward hers, she stops him

DARIA: Uh-uh. I'm a good girl. I don't kiss on a first date.

beat, he laughs, she laughs

ELWOOD: Wooo. That was –

DARIA: I know, right.

ELWOOD: Woah, got me one helluva headrush.

DARIA: Good, 'at's good, 'cause now I've got your attention, how's about you gimme some of them there pills you seem so keen on keeping your mitts on.

ELWOOD: Oh I don't know about that.

DARIA: No?

she twists her grip on his genitalia, he yelps, it treads the fine line between erotic and aggressive

Come on, you saying I didn't satisfy you honey.

ELWOOD: Oh no no no no I ain't saying that.

DARIA: Well, reckon I must've earned me a few a' those, at the very least.

ELWOOD: Oh, I don't know.

DARIA: You don't?

she tightens her grip

That's weird.

ELWOOD: I s'pose.

DARIA: So how's about it then?

ELWOOD: Well, how's about you let go of my – how's about you let go of me first?

DARIA: How's about I don't?

ELWOOD: Wait a minute, you want one or not?

DARIA: How's about I hold your little fellas hostage 'til I get what I want –

ELWOOD: Well, how'm I s'posed to get 'em if you're –

DARIA: Got two hands, don't you?

she twists a little more, ELWOOD's light flashes orange

ELWOOD: Okay okay okay okay.

DARIA: Really wanna watch that heart-rate a' yours, I can hear it from here.

beat

ELWOOD: Close your eyes.

DARIA: What? Why?!

ELWOOD: 'cause I don't want you spotting my hiding spot is why, now close your eyes.

DARIA: No fucking way. How do I know you ain't gonna club me over the head with something –

ELWOOD: I'm hardly in a position to do that, am I?

DARIA: Yeah, well I don't trust you.

ELWOOD: WILL YOU JUST CLOSE YOUR EYES?

DARIA: *(tightening)* I don't think you're in a position to negotiate, Elwood

ELWOOD: Alright, okay, Jesus.

he reaches and retrieves the pills from their hiding place, he pops the top, she holds out her open palm, and he empties one or two into her hand

DARIA: You for real?

ELWOOD: What?

DARIA: Keep 'em coming.

ELWOOD: Are you kidding?

DARIA: Do I look like I'm kidding?

ELWOOD: I dunno –

DARIA: *(twisting)* Does it *feel* like I'm kidding?

ELWOOD: AH! AH! AH!

DARIA: Two weeks to the big cut ain't it?

ELWOOD: So?

DARIA: So gimme two weeks' worth.

ELWOOD: You have *got* to be kidding me?

DARIA: Do I really need to repeat myself?

ELWOOD: No, okay, okay, okay.

he empties more pills into her hand

DARIA: 'at's better. Now what do I do with 'em?

ELWOOD: Swallow 'em a'course, what do you *think* / you do –

DARIA: I know that dumbass but when –

ELWOOD: Soon as you wake up, that way it'll hit you just in time for morning drills.

DARIA: *(twisting)* You ain't fucking with me now are you?

ELWOOD: Swear, I swear, Jesus, better on an empty stomach, comes on harder and quicker that way.

DARIA: …

ELWOOD: Now, can I have my pecker back.

DARIA: Thought you'd never ask.

she releases him, wipes her hand on his blanket and returns to her side of the room, he rolls over onto his side and caresses himself

DARIA: Pleasure doing business.

ELWOOD: Shit, that really smarts.

DARIA: Go to sleep, Elwood.

ELWOOD: Might not be able to have kids 'cause a' you.

DARIA: Prolly've turned out retards anyway.

ELWOOD: I'm serious. And you should know, I snuck those in up my ass by the way!

DARIA: Mmm, sweet.

ELWOOD: You think I'm joking?

DARIA: Go to sleep, Elwood.

ELWOOD: 'cause I ain't joking.

DARIA: Did you hear what I said?

ELWOOD: Well…

DARIA: *Go to sleep.*

ELWOOD rolls away from her, DARIA sits on the edge of her bed

she looks down at the pills in her hand

she think about where to keep them, after a moment she secretes them somewhere on her person she lies back on the bed

after a beat…

DARIA: Elwood, knock the light off.

beat

(propping herself up on her elbow) Elwood.

she notices that ELWOOD's breathing has become slower and heavier and that he's sleeping

a thought hits her

she gingerly gets up, trying to not let the mattress creak too much

she tip-toes over to ELWOOD's side of the room

he snores, beat

she scoots down and slowly slides ELWOOD's game console out from under the end of his pillow, trying her best not to wake him

as she pulls the end of it from under the pillow he turns in his sleep so he's directly facing her

beat

she flicks the light off and retreats to her side of the room and gets into bed

she switches the game on, it make a loud noise, ELWOOD stirs

she adjusts the volume to its lowest possible setting

her face is illuminated by the game

she removes a pill from her pocket, looks at it, puts it on her tongue and swallows it

she begins to play, at first she is clumsy, her brow furrowed

soon she becomes more and more adept

her fingers skip faster and faster over the buttons, her face relaxes

streaks of light from the game shoot across her face

it should feel like she's moving faster and faster

sound of chaos

light and dark compete for dominance

out of this...

the restaurant

CLARA finishes writing on the napkin with her lipstick and slides it back across the table toward GREG and immediately proceeds to freshen up her lips with it, maybe using something on the table to check her reflection

silence

GREG: What is this?

CLARA: I'm sure you think you have a comfortable life. But everything is relative. It can always be more comfortable.

beat

GREG: That's –

CLARA: More money than you can visualise? I know, right? *(with a giggle)* I mean, what does that amount of money even look like?

GREG: This is –

CLARA: What we will pay you up front. A first instalment. It can be in your bank account in a half hour. Just say the word.

GREG: Wait –

CLARA: And if you wanna talk bottom line – *(with a casual waft of her hand)* pfff, I don't know, double it, add a zero and you're probably in the right ballpark.

beat, he looks over his shoulder and leans in over the table toward her

GREG: This has to be –

CLARA: You don't need to whisper, Greg. We're all on the same side here.

GREG: *(looking over his shoulder again)* But this is –

CLARA: *(wearily)* Will you please stop that?

GREG: Stop what, I wasn't –

CLARA: Looking over your shoulder. You look like you're planning to run off without picking up the check. It's embarrassing, have some composure, please.

she finishes touching up her lips

GREG: I'm going to need some time –

CLARA: *(negative)* Uh-uh.

GREG: I'm sorry?

CLARA: No you're not.

GREG: Just a couple of –

CLARA: Not possible.

GREG: But this is –

CLARA: Believe me, I'd give you the weekend if I could, I really would, but time is ticking on this.

GREG: 24 hours, I just need 24 hours to –

CLARA: Afraid not, I'm going to have to push you for an answer.

GREG: Now?

CLARA: Right.

GREG: Right now?! You have to be kidding.

CLARA: Do I look like I'm kidding?

pause

GREG: *(taking in the figure on the napkin)* You want to know whether I'm in or out.

CLARA: *(with a wry smile)* I want to know whether you're with us or against us.

sound of chaos

light and dark compete for dominance

the dorm room

ELWOOD is pacing, DARIA sat on her bunk

ELWOOD: A hundred spots! In't that what they said?

DARIA: Y'I heard –

ELWOOD: A hundred?! That is what they said isn't it?

DARIA: Y'I heard, Elwood, we all did –

ELWOOD: But that / means –

DARIA: I know what it –

ELWOOD: That means –

DARIA: I know what it means okay so –

ELWOOD: Half of us, shipped outta here, half of us, in one big –

DARIA: Y'I can do the math Elwood, could do that one in kindergarten –

ELWOOD: But I was, I mean, I was counting on –

DARIA: What, counting on / what?

ELWOOD: Mean when they said 'final cut' I thought –

DARIA: Well, you thought wrong din't you.

ELWOOD: But I thought –

DARIA: What, you thought what?

ELWOOD: I dunno but shit I din't think they meant half of us!

beat

You seem pretty relaxed about all this.

DARIA: That's one way a' looking at it?

ELWOOD: And what's the other way?

DARIA: That you're pretty worked up about it.

69

ELWOOD: Right now, we stay where we are on the
leaderboard, we're both going home tomorrow –

DARIA: I ain't stupid –

ELWOOD: You do get that don't you?

DARIA: Yeah well getting all worked up over it isn't going to /
help you any, is it?

ELWOOD: Have you *seen* my averages? Have you? Have you
seen my scores?

DARIA: Seen a lot worse.

ELWOOD: Yeah, from lard-ass no-hopers who right now are
back at home carving a nice groove for themselves in their
beat-up sofas.

DARIA: Yeah, and you ain't like them.

ELWOOD: Don't look that way –

DARIA: Just hit a sticky patch is all.

ELWOOD: Right now, I'm following 'em, right out the door

DARIA: *Yeah, you're prolly right.*

beat

ELWOOD: *What did you say?*

DARIA: Said you're prolly right, if you're going to stick with
this attitude, which totally stinks by the way, then yeah
you prolly are gonna screw this up tomorrow so –

ELWOOD: Wow, thanks –

DARIA: Well, it's true –

ELWOOD: Jeez –

DARIA: Sayin' it like I see it.

ELWOOD: That's a great help!

DARIA: All I'm saying's / if you go into tomorrow thinking you're gonna get cut // then that's prolly what's gonna /// happen.

ELWOOD: / Thanks!

// Wow.

/// Thanks a million –

DARIA: You ain't hearing me, / you gotta adjust your attitude.

ELWOOD: Oh, I hear you, I hear you loud and clear –

DARIA: *Look.* You're jiggered is all.

ELWOOD: What does that even mean?

DARIA: Your nerves, they're shot to hell. 'at's obvious. Maybe you shoulda been taking it easy with them pills all this time.

ELWOOD: Oh yeah?

DARIA: You been popping 'em like they're breath mints.

ELWOOD: What do you even know anyway, what do you actually know about anything, 'cause suddenly it's like you're some sorta expert or something, is that what's happened 'cause –

DARIA: I know enough to know you prolly shouldn't be gunning one a' those things after every meal.

ELWOOD: 's 'at right?

DARIA: My advice? Right now? Take a breath.

ELWOOD: Take a breath! Breathe! Those are your words of wisdom? Well, thanks for that. That's real fuckin' useful! Say, did I even ask for your advice?

DARIA: *No you didn't but you've been snivelling on about it for the best part of an hour so I'm just tryna get you to shut the hell up!*

silence

ELWOOD: No need to chew my head off, shit!

DARIA: Me chew *your* head off – are you kidding me?

ELWOOD: What?

DARIA: I said '*me* chew *your* –

ELWOOD: Okay, yeah, maybe I, maybe it was me that, yeah, I, maybe I am a bit hyped.

DARIA: You don't say. Shit.

ELWOOD: Okay, maybe you was right –

DARIA: Fuckin-a I'm right! Now, will you listen to me, like actually listen, for just one second?

beat

ELWOOD: I'm listening.

DARIA: You need to relax. You carry on like this, come tomorrow you're gonna be a basket case, then it ain't gonna matter 'bout your averages or your scores or anything –

ELWOOD: Easy to say that, 'relax'

DARIA: Will you listen, *will you?*

ELWOOD: …

DARIA: Way I see it, it's prolly best you had the week you had. Prolly means you're gonna peak at the right time. 's way I'd be looking at it anyway.

ELWOOD: Easy for you to say, if anyone's peaking at the right time –

DARIA: Hey, I'm heading home tomorrow, I know I am. Lucky I made it *this* far. Had a good run but I've hit my ceiling, I know that.

Only way I'll be here after tomorrow is if Larson goes on some kinda 'Battle Royale' killing spree over breakfast.

beat, ELWOOD lightens up slightly

But you, you worked hard for this. You've just gone missing is all. Find your groove again you'll be back in business –

ELWOOD: Yeah…maybe…

DARIA: I'm telling you. Get focussed, sure, but first you gotta relax.

ELWOOD: Maybe you're right.

DARIA: Sure I am.

beat

ELWOOD: Say, why you being like this?

DARIA: What you mean?

ELWOOD: Nice to me or whatever.

DARIA: Hey, don't go thinking I'm doing this for you, not *just* for you anyways.

ELWOOD: What's 'at mean?

DARIA: Want *you* to calm the hell down so's *I* can get some peace and quiet.

ELWOOD smiles

Plus.

ELWOOD: What?

DARIA: Nothing.

ELWOOD: What is it?

DARIA: Dunno

Maybe I come to terms with something.

ELWOOD: And wha's 'at?

DARIA: That I don't think I can do this.

beat

ELWOOD: You mean – ?

DARIA: What they'll need me to do…that I won't be able to live with that.

ELWOOD: Right…so why come this / far.

DARIA: 'cause every day I'm in here is a day I'm not out there.

beat

ELWOOD: What'll you do…when you're back out there I mean –

DARIA: Fuck it, I'll survive…always find a way…

silence, ELWOOD sits on his bed, he lies back, he tries to breathe deeply, he sits back up, he's twitchy and fidgety

ELWOOD: 's easier said than done.

DARIA: What is?

ELWOOD: Kicking back, 'm all wired, head's all –

DARIA: C'mere.

ELWOOD: What?

DARIA: Come over here.

ELWOOD: Why?

DARIA: Just come over here will you –

ELWOOD: Yeah, but, what for?

DARIA: 'n stop askin' so many questions.

he does, standing in front of her

ELWOOD: Okay. So. What?

DARIA: Turn around. Sit.

ELWOOD: …

DARIA: Sit down for chrissakes.

he sits on the floor, between her legs
she puts her hands on his shoulders

ELWOOD: Hey, what are you –

DARIA: Relax! Jeez. Tryna do you a favour here.

she starts to massage his shoulders

DARIA: There, ain't that better.

ELWOOD: Hell, that feels good

DARIA: There you go.

Jeez, 's like tryna massage a rock.

she finds a knot, struggles with it

Take your shirt off a minute.

ELWOOD: What?

DARIA: Your shirt, take it off so's I can –

ELWOOD: I don't –

DARIA: I ain't gonna try it on, Elwood! Just can't get my thumbs in there. 'f you take it off I can –

ELWOOD: I don't know –

DARIA: Fine, leave it on, just tryna help is all –

ELWOOD: Okay.

he takes the t-shirt off, revealing a tattoo on his shoulder blade of the name 'maggie'

he slings the t-shirt on the bed next to DARIA

beat

DARIA: Sick ink. 'maggie'. Who's 'at, your girl?

ELWOOD: Something like that.

DARIA: 's a nice name.

ELWOOD: Yeah?

DARIA: It is!

She pretty?

75

ELWOOD: She's my ma.

beat

DARIA: 'at's sweet.

ELWOOD: *(jokingly)* Fuck off.

DARIA: It is, I ain't screwing with you.

ELWOOD: Okay…

she continues to massage him in silence

Tchula.

DARIA: What?

ELWOOD: Tchula, Mississippi. 's where I'm from. You asked did'n you, before, when we first got here, and I did'n say nothing but now I'm telling you so now you know, 's Tchula. Tchula, Mississippi.

You know it?

DARIA: *(negative)* Uh-uh.

ELWOOD: Got no reason to, it's a hole.

Tell you something, sure as hell don't wanna go back there.

beat

DARIA: What *you* gonna do, when you're out there I mean.

ELWOOD: 'at all depends, don't it –

DARIA: Guess.

ELWOOD: Whether I got dollars in my pocket.

DARIA: Right.

beat

ELWOOD: I'd start again, I reckon.

Build me a big ole house, middle of nowhere, just the way I wanted it. Good, solid wood. Strong, you know. And there wouldn't be nobody around for miles. And I mean *miles*. You'd look in any direction and you wouldn't see another person, not one. And there'd be enough room for everyone – me, my ma, brothers, sisters, aunts, uncles, cousins, hell the whole gang of us. Dozens 'a rooms! And no one there to bother us about this or that, no one, not ever.

And I'd...I guess I'd work the fields, Yeah 'at's what I'd do. Old school. 'cause the soil, it'd be good – *good* soil. And yeah, I'd grow stuff, rear animals, the whole nine yards, we'd do it all ourselves, live off the land, We wouldn't be relying on nobody. No, sir. And the water'd be clean – hell, I'd forgotten what clean water tasted like 'til I came in here.

And it'd be mine. I'd own it. Wouldn't owe nobody for it and nobody'd be trying to take it from me. Wouldn't be scrabbling 'round in the dirt for nothing no more...

beat

And my ma, when she dies, 'cause she prolly ain't got long left, I know that, but when she does...she'll go with a smile on her face. Just calm, comfortable... happy.

beat

Sounds corny, right? Ah, I don't give a shit.

DARIA: No, it sounds –

ELWOOD: Yeah?

DARIA: It does.

ELWOOD: Well, 'at's what I'd do I reckon.

Yeah...

DARIA has stopped massaging him. She has got lost in his fantasy, she's glassy eyed

silence

You done?

DARIA: Yeah…

ELWOOD: Boy, 'at feels good. Think you might just have the golden touch. My t-shirt there?

DARIA: Sure.

she pulls the t-shirt into her lap

beat

ELWOOD: You okay?

DARIA: I'm fine –

ELWOOD: 'cause you sound a little –

DARIA swiftly loops the t-shirt around his neck and begins to strangle him, his hands leap to his throat initially, then they scrabble to try and grab her, he belts her in the mouth, she panics and pulls harder, he scrabbles even more, grabbing at her

For a brief moment he arches his head back and they look each other square in the eye

She pushes a knee into the middle of his back pushing him facedown onto the floor

he continues to jerk around like a trapped insect

his light flashes orange and there's a loud beep

she pulls harder with the t-shirt and pushes harder with the knee in his back

he grabs her thigh, then her arm, and tries unsuccessfully to grab higher

the orange alarm signal beeps again, louder this time, closely followed by her light changing to orange and beeping loudly

she tightens the grip around his neck and clamps his head to the ground with her other hand before bashing his head against the ground repeatedly, it's frantic and violent

he's still, blood starts to seep out from underneath his head there is stillness and silence for a brief moment, the only sound is the sound of her breathlessness

then…

his light turns red and a piercing sound is emitted

she panics and scrabbles across the floor towards the back wall, her nose and mouth are bloodied

there's the sound of boots and voices at a distance down the corridor

she scrabbles to get his games console and his stash of pills, she hides them under her pillow as the door is opened the light from outside in the corridor illuminates both DARIA sat on the floor and the body of ELWOOD splayed in front of her.

she spits blood out onto the floor, as her breathing returns to normal she slowly gets up and stands at her full height

there's a look in her eyes that we haven't seen before

sound of chaos

light and dark compete for dominance

THE PROGRAM

you have all earned the right to be stood here in front a' me

you have all earned the opportunity to dig yourself out of the shit-pit you have found yourselves in

this is where stuff gets interesting forget about points this is about dollars

everything you destroy is monetised

your task is simple flatten anything that looks man-made your pilots will do the rest

keep it simple keep it neat do not stray from your remit

you do not get points for artistic interpretation you get points for accuracy you get points for efficiency

missiles cost money people

folk I represent the folk who will be paying you they like money

they like money an awful lot
they don't like spending more money than they have to
they like to spend money and get a fuck-ton of it back for
their dollar-investment

light fades up on DARIA standing alone in the space

*she is now dressed in in a blue-grey flight-suit and boots, she stands
to attention*

take a look at the screens in front of you
an entire virtual world mapped directly on top of ours with
millimetre precision
every square inch of that world correlates exactly with a
square inch of this one.
the geography, the names, the borders all omitted to protect
you to distance you
the controls are identical to your training simulations
think of it as a game
think of it as a video game
think of it as the mother of all video games

–

happy hunting everybody.
I have one last thing to say to you
this is no longer a simulation this is for real

over the THE PROGRAM's text, lines of light streak across DARIA

the streaks of light move both horizontally and vertically

they start to become more frequent and slowly start to form gridlines

*the gridlines increase in speed and intensity until DARIA is drowned
in light and noise*

out of this...

the restaurant, as before

beat, as long as it takes

GREG looks up from the napkin and offers his hand

CLARA smiles and takes it

CLARA: Well, well. You put up a good fight.

GREG: This is –

CLARA: Congratulations. You've made the right decision.

GREG: I sure hope so.

CLARA: You're nervous.

GREG: What?

CLARA: You grip too hard. Clear giveaway. You need to work on that.

In the meantime, hey, let's drink to the fuck-ton of money you just made yourself.

she clinks his glass, beat

GREG: So…what happens now?

CLARA: My people have already made a number of determinations. Everything is in hand, wheels are turning as we speak. You're one of the final pieces of the puzzle.

GREG: Right –

CLARA: When the time is right we'll flatten them, and that's where you'll come in.

GREG: Flatten?

CLARA: Right.

GREG: Flatten what?

beat

CLARA: The cities, Greg. The cities.

GREG: But I thought –

CLARA: Yeah, gotta knock the old ones down first though, right! Make ourselves a little room.

beat

GREG: But you said –

CLARA: *(coquettishly)* I know.

GREG: You said that –

CLARA: I know what I said, Greg. It was me that said it after all.

GREG: You said this wasn't a, a –

CLARA: I did, and it's not.

GREG: Not in the Middle East, nothing like that, that's what you said –

CLARA: That is exactly what I said –

GREG: Right!

CLARA: And it's not. I didn't lie to you Greg.

GREG: Then where?

CLARA: Oh, don't look like that. Those eyes.

GREG: *I asked you where, God dammit?*

    beat

    she smiles, she sips

CLARA: Mmm – meant to say, I'd stay in New York this weekend if I were you.

GREG: What?

CLARA: Your plans. I'd stay in New York.

GREG: Why?

CLARA: I just would. Philadelphia? I don't know, I gotta feeling there won't be much to see.

GREG: …

CLARA: *(sigh)* Read between the lines, Greg. Right here in this room is the safest place to be right now. And that way you can enjoy the light show. Front row seats.

beat

GREG: I don't –

beat

Are you – ?

beat

Are you saying what I think you're – ?

CLARA: Ten cities to begin with. A statement of intent. And if things don't change…then I guess we'll be forced to move the parameters of our program.

GREG: You're insane –

CLARA: This country's sick, Greg. It's sick, and when something is sick it either needs curing or it needs putting down, and one of those things is a darn sight easier than the other.

GREG: You are, you're –

CLARA: We're going to build something new. You're going to help us build it. You'll help us build it just the way we want it.

GREG: You're – you're out of your mind.

CLARA: Quite possibly. But when did that ever stop anyone from doing anything.

GREG: But what – what about – ?

CLARA: *(on a tiny laugh)* The people?

beat

(she shrugs) Pfff, I'm going to hell but I'm fine with it.

GREG: I think I'd like to leave now.

CLARA: Yeah that won't be possible.

GREG: I did not sign up for this –

CLARA: You signed up for this when you stepped through that door.

GREG: No –

CLARA: Why don't you sit down. Why don't you lower your voice. You're making an exhibition of yourself.

GREG: No, you know what –

CLARA: Fine, stand up. Leave. This thing is happening, with or without you. Choice is do you wanna be up here with us looking down…or do you wanna be down there with them looking up?

CLARA's cell 'phone vibrates, she checks it

GREG: You people, you can't seriously think you'll get away with this.

CLARA: *(putting her cell 'phone back down)* We already have.

beat

So what's it gonna be?

silence, stillness

eventually he sits, poleaxed

'at a boy.

Say, you're looking a little grey around the gills, Greg.

No point getting squeamish. It's just business.

Relax, it always hurts the first time.

she takes the olive out of her martini

You remember your first olive? Tasted like crap, am I right? But in time you grew to love it. You acquired a taste. Same as your first coffee, your first beer…

Same with this. You'll grow to love it. You'll have to. You have no choice now.

she pulls the olive off the cocktail stick with her teeth carefully and then devours it

after some time

GREG: I – I think I'd like to call my wife.

CLARA: Sure you would.

GREG: Hear her voice.

CLARA: Yeah, in a while. She's not going anywhere.

he nods to himself

beat

GREG: So, what – what happens now?

CLARA: Now?

Well, I don't know about you but I'm ravenous.

Dessert?

light and dark compete for dominance

the chaos swells

we catch a fleeting glimpse of DARIA, she gasps as if waking from a nightmare

everything is swallowed in light and sound and chaos

then…

silence, darkness

WWW.OBERONBOOKS.COM

Follow us on Twitter @oberonbooks
& Facebook @OberonBooksLondon